GODLESS BUT LOYAL TO HEAVEN

GODLESS BUT LOYAL TO Heaven

stories

Richard Van Camp

ENFIELD &WIZENTY

Enfield & Wizenty
(An imprint of Great Plains Publications)
345-955 Portage Avenue
Winnipeg, MB R3G 0P9
www.greatplains.mb.ca

Great Plains Publications gratefully acknowledges the financial support provided for its publishing program by the Government of Canada through the Canada Book Fund; the Canada Council for the Arts; the Province of Manitoba through the Book Publishing Tax Credit and the Book Publisher Marketing Assistance Program; and the Manitoba Arts Council.

Design & Typography by Relish New Brand Experience Inc.
Printed in Canada by Friesens
First Edition

LIBRARY AND ARCHIVES CANADA CATALOGUING IN PUBLICATION

Van Camp, Richard, 1971-
    Godless but loyal to heaven / Richard Van Camp.

Short stories.
Issued also in electronic formats.
ISBN 978-1-926531-56-4

    I. Title.

PS8593.A5376G63 2012   C813'.54   C2012-903583-1

FSC
www.fsc.org
MIX
Paper from
responsible sources
FSC® C016245

ENVIRONMENTAL BENEFITS STATEMENT

Great Plains Publications saved the following resources by printing the pages of this book on chlorine free paper made with 100% post-consumer waste.

TREES	WATER	ENERGY	SOLID WASTE	GREENHOUSE GASES
6	2,606	2	165	578
FULLY GROWN	GALLONS	MILLION BTUs	POUNDS	POUNDS

Environmental impact estimates were made using the Environmental Paper Network Paper Calculator. For more information visit www.papercalculator.org.

Dedicated with love to Keavy Martin

Table of Contents

On the Wings of this Prayer

THERE ARE TWO STORIES MY GREAT-GRANDFATHER TOLD ME. HE said a long time ago before *them* — the Shark Throats, he called them, during the time of the warming world — there was a family in the way of the Tar Sands of Alberta. One day as the mother was gathering water, she stepped on teeth in the ice and muskeg. The jaws of an old man, a trapper, had thawed enough to bite her. She ran but she did not escape. The woman got very sick: buttons of pus boiling through a body rash, the paling, her hands hooking to claws. She asked her husband to bring her glass after glass of water. She was thirsty and panting. He kept bringing her more, yet she never drank. She said something was coming through her. Something starving.

Her voice then turned to a low growl as she began to rock for hours hissing, "Kill me now. Kill me now or I'll kill you all before the sunrise. Do it, do it if you love me. Kill me please. Your meat is magnificent and what roars in your veins is calling me. It's calling me to drink you open and warm me so sweetly. Oh let me start with your scars and scabs. Let me. Let me taste you. You'd let me if you love me."

As her husband returned with help, she snapped at the air with her teeth and rasped before striking out wildly at all of them with her nails. After they subdued her, she begged again for all of them to kill her — before the sunrise, she insisted. They tied her fists and feet and ran for more help. When they returned, she was gone. She'd torn her binding and fled, but the strangest thing — the oddest thing — were the glasses of water he'd brought her. They'd all turned to ice. Her husband never saw his wife again. They think she was the first and they say she is still here as their queen, that she gives birth to them through her mouth. Hatching them through her over and over. More and more. *The boiled faces*, we call them — *zombies*, our son said — and they remember faces.

The Tar Sands of Alberta had tailing ponds and excavators, and I am sure those teeth belonged to that old trapper who lived out there before them. That old man, no matter how much money the oil companies offered him, would not budge, so they built and dug around him. He quit coming to town. There was a family who went to visit him, to bring him supplies, but he had changed. He had gone to white and had eaten his own lips and fingers. He had stepped in bear traps spiked to the floors on purpose. He could still speak and said the devil was in him now and that they had to cut him up. They had to burn his heart and scatter his ashes after they cut his head off.

They did everything he asked them to, but the land was uncovered and turned for years by excavators, tractors and the curiosity of men. We think those machines must have moved the heavy rocks that covered his limbs. We think his fingers were able to crawl back to the torso and legs and head. We don't think they burnt his heart to ashes because they saw him again and he killed many, many people by biting at them. Burning, cutting, stabbing, shooting — all of it was wasted until his family heard of him walking again, so they told the people how to stop him. And that's how we knew. That was how we knew to stop the boiled faces with the old ways.

There is a ritual to things now: a lunge shot with the Decapitator through the skull. It's a longer harpoon with a cross-axe on the hilt to ram and split the skull so zombies can't grab you. It detaches so you can begin chopping. Only good one on one. Useless against many. Scramble the brains. This blinds and confuses the body. With a quick twist, the top blade comes off to free the axe. Then you hack the right arm (the reaching one) off before the left (the grabbing one) — is to be cut. Then you take the right leg and the left before cutting the heart out. As the heart is burnt with a sharpened flare, the Known People turn, look away and chant in Apache, *"Deeyá, Deeyá"* for "Leave, leave." We believe that what is left of the soul still rises and the spirit of the person inside will know to look away, as well, so it doesn't need to see what has happened to its body. There is respect and fear in this. Then we bury the limbs far apart and weigh them down with stones. The Known People buried everything and everyone pointing north, even though we've all seen some of them come back marked and scored. (Are they unburying each other or themselves?)

I can still speak Dogrib, me, but Apache is the common tongue for the Known People—or it was before the three of us were banished. For some reason, when the Hair Eaters come, it slows them when you sing or talk to them or chant in the first tongue. It's like they're listening. They weaken when you chant and that's when you take them.

All those old movies were true: body shots are wasted. Even with a shattered spine, they crawl. You'd think by now we'd be used to this, but they've a hot, sweet smell like dead fish that turns your stomach when they near. We then burn their limbs to ashes and scatter them. This is why the air tastes as it does. Their wild, rolling cry is used to paralyze, but it is not as strong as their mother's. I heard it a few times in the sky and felt the strength leave my legs, but our drums drown them out. If you drum you can stop their mewling cry, turn it to ice in their throats. Also, our little group has discovered that The Boiled Faces are terrified of butterflies. They run screaming—as if set to flames—when they see a butterfly and that's why we've camped here. Also, this is why we bottle them. All it takes is one butterfly and when one runs, they all do. It is hilarious. I laugh every time I see this. I wish I could have done The Butterfly Test to the Known People. I bet they would have all run away. I would have laughed so hard I would have thrown myself upon a Decapitator throat-first and not come back.

The zombies took our dogs first, systematically and determinedly. Once the dogs were gone we were blind and deaf to them. I miss the dogs. I can't even think of their names or I will weep. A wise hunter looked where they looked, always, and dogs always know more about storms than humans. And we used the old ways when we took one down with the dogs: we poked their halfway-human-and-mean-as-starving eyes out so they wouldn't see you the next time. We sliced the tips of their ears off and hung them high so they wouldn't hear you the next time, but they do. The new ones can.

I hear of things in the ravaged south (no word from the west), but they, I hope, are rumours: death cults who eat or rape the Shark Throats for power, building sod huts and using their stomach linings for windows. In the east, thousands of people wait with their eyes closed in fields to be taken at once so they can come back to roam together. And they say the new generation of the Boiled Faces can sing themselves back together. Let us pray that this is not true.

Here in the north, the Known People dressed their children in rabbit fur and seal skins. I'm not sure if I agree with the practice of sewing bones under the skin, but I saw that most youths' faces were tattooed in the way of *Kakiniit*, ghost marks in memory of the One Sun. The Known People were greedy to learn our songs for the slowing.

If you are reading this, please know that I tell you these things because I love you and wish for the world a better way. I have sent this back to tell you this, my ancestor: the Tar Sands are ecocide. They will bring Her back. In both stories, it is the Tar Sands to blame. This is how the Wheetago will return.

As far as we can tell, the exact pinpoint is around the time when they transport one atom from one part of the world to the other. This has something to do with all of everything during your time. You must stop the Tar Sands. At all costs. If you read this, there is still a spirit with a starving heart there. Waiting to be resurrected.

I've seen them chase down an older couple as they ran in deep, black snow. One Shark Throat—a newer, smaller one, one with a long beak and hooks for thumbs, raced ahead and circled back, floating over the land. He cut his way into their stomachs with his claws. The elders' stomachs opened like mouths and out poured their guts.

The larger Hair Eaters began to eat their unravelling intestines as they stumbled away. It was a game to them. The younger one gripped and squeezed their grey, steaming leashes as the half-alive elders tried to scream, but all that came out of their mouths was slop. The younger one began to slowly braid their guts together while pulling them closer, nearer, playing with its food. The others feasted. The younger Hair Eater looked up and saw me and pointed but the others kept gorging. It opened its beak and let out a cry as it started to run towards me. The cry tangled my wings. Their sound: it rings through what is hollow inside you. It finds your marrow and squeezes it to weaken you. And I think once their song touches you, they can hear what you are thinking.

At night, when I sleepwalk, my soul leaves my body and I fly. I could always fly and that was why I had to save Thinksawhile. I spied on the leaders of the Known People. They were boiling and eating old moccasins and mukluks and they were talking of having him fall through the ice and eating him frozen. This explained our last few meals. Oh Creator, the things we've done to survive. That night, we took the boy and his computers and left, travelling downwind, upwind and though the fog. East. Always moving east. Watching the skies for ravens as ravens follow them for what's left.

Four Blankets Woman covered my eyes with ash. "So the new ones can see you."

"Heh eh," I said. "They are getting smarter, crueler."

She rubbed my back with palms of yarrow. "We need new medicine."

"You know what was beautiful?" I said. "Those elders they tore apart, they never stopped holding hands or trying to…."

"Shhh," she said as she rested on my chest. "I know how to beat them now."

I turned. "How?"

"The new ones have beaks."

"Heh eh."

"And it has a tongue to direct sound?" I nodded.

"I will chant on this to see."

The next morning I woke to find she'd tattooed my eyelids with syllabics. She'd also sliced her left breast open and marked our Decapitators with strange symbols of whips and dots. "For your weapons and wings," she said.

I closed my eyes and looked at the fire to see this magic again. "Are these from heaven?"

"*In le*," she said, stirring broth. "*Gah*. The Rabbit. There are only two left and they have passed their medicine to me. They told me how to beat them and the Bitch." Thinksawhile looked up from his computer.

"This will cost us one of our lives. We have to choose carefully."

Four Blankets knew the way of the four winds. I had seen her part the clouds. She knew which root and moss to braid to make wick for cooking and heat. Her medicine was rabbit medicine. When she was thirteen, she saved the life of a doe. In turn, she was given Gah medicine. Four Blankets Woman had tattooed our tongues, so the Hair Eaters could not hear us speak. Not even in this dream.

She ran soot down her nose. "Whoever we choose will suffer, but it is the only way." The boy was young, weak. I had a blown right knee and couldn't stop talking in my sleep.

"We choose tonight," she said and left to slice her arm to ribbons. This was the cost of a Dream Thrower.

Thinksawhile went back to his computer. "I have an idea," he said. "A way to stop this. A way to undo all that's been done."

I began to braid my hair. "Tell me," I said. And he did.

Before we fled, the sick cooked for us. The sick chanted for us. Scouts left. Our son vanished. Women gave birth to things that were killed immediately (except redheads), and there was a low growl from the cancered earth that trembled us. All Known Elders turned blind. What the last hunter brought was a hand that could be bear with an eye sewn backwards into the palm. Could be human, could be them.

Knuckle sockets sucked dry. I touched one and singed my finger. It burns at night when I dream.

Now the air is loaded with ash that coats us and the wings of the butterflies, and my dreams. My dreams.

The Hair Eaters have eaten all the caribou, moose, bear, fox, wolf, bison, buffalo and everything under the earth here. We are too scared to check nets as they feast on our catch underwater and wait for boats. All we have left are creatures of the air: ducks and ptarmigan, geese, swans. We eat roots pretending they are what we used to love.

This message comes from the future. From our Dream Thrower. Remember, there is a hard way and an easy way: stop the Tar Sands and that old man's body from waking up. He—not she—is the beginning of the end. May your children—our ancestors—not know a time of being born hunted as we are all hunted now.

As for us, our season's done, and I miss smiling at my memories. It's getting colder now. Soon the fist of the sun will surrender to frost. We see it on the lower mountains across the way. Soon the butterflies will leave (where do they sleep at night?) and they will find us. They say some humans are farming other humans and making deals with the Hair Eaters. At night, when I lower myself to the cooling earth, as I breathe through my palms to cool my roaring head, my finger burns. I think this is how they are tracking us.

I heard a story once. It warmed even the hearts of the Known People. It was a story outside of Fort Providence. The buffalo ran with two giant horses, two Clydesdales: one white, one brown. When you approached the herd you could clap your hands and the buffalo would look one way, the horses the other. Wolves and the zombies could not come near for trampling and goring. I sometimes think about how the horses and buffalo adopted each other. What was their ritual for each other? I told that story the second night after moving with the Known People, and they marvelled until hunters from that region reported that two giant horse skulls burned among the mountains of bones. They also spoke of lakes now, filled with humans swimming in their own blood. Hundreds of women, men, children, elders, harpooned and buoyed by jerry cans to keep them floating. "It's the adrenaline," a sharpshooter who got away said. "It sweetens our blood. They keep us terrified and once we die, they tear into us. They just keep adding more and more people to these lakes. There were lines of people for miles, as far as we could see."

I saw a grey whale once, rolling in shallow water. Hundreds of Hair Eaters poured over the body biting, ripping at the barnacles and sea lice. Others clawed and reached into the eyes and blow-holes. One dove into its mouth. Then others. Then more and more. It thrashed and couldn't get away. The Shark Throats ate their way from the inside until I could see its skeleton. I watched a mile away and heard it scream. Their cries are supposed to be subsonic but I heard it. I still hear it.

I've seen a pack of Hair Eaters down a pack of bison in slush. The lead bull flipped in the air as the opposing Hair Eaters forked to cut him off. As he flipped in the air, two were upon him ripping and tearing at his belly and balls. He was hollowed out completely by the time he landed, still kicking.

We wish you luck. The future is a curse. There are no human trails left. I was born running from them as they are born starving and hunting for us. Now, we carry on in fever. We carry on for you and what you do next.

Four Blankets Woman has thrown two dreams now: one for you and the other to prove it. In your time, Taiwan will shut down its biggest highway for seven suns to allow for the safe passage of one million butterflies. If this is so, you will know this warning to be true.

I pray you remember this when you wake up.

You must remember this.

You must stop the Tar Sands. Do not bring cancer to our Mother. Do not unleash them.

On the wings of this atomized prayer, we reach to you with all we have left.

Now, they have expanded their range to the fullest here and are crossing the ice of time to reach you—you who live in the time before the sun twins, when fish only had one mouth, when moose knew who they were.

You *can* change the future.

Now wake up.

The Fleshing

"YOU SHOULD BE SLEEPING," EHTSE SAID AS HE DROPPED ME OFF in his Suburban. I rubbed my eyes.

"Can't." Those damned dreams, I thought, and that voice: *they can remember faces*. What the hell did that mean?

I was too lazy to walk, and there was no way I'd carry all this meat here by myself.

Grandpa eyed the principal's house and I could almost read his thoughts: *all this money but the Spruces don't hunt*. I wondered if he thought, deep down, that this made the Spruces poorer than us. We smelled like bush: dry meat and smoke. I caught it on my collar and loved the aroma. Ehtsi had just made a fresh bunch of *boogoo*, caribou dry meat, and I was just itching for a Coke. I loved to drink ice cold Coke while ripping into dry meat. Plus, it would keep me awake.

"Thanks again for the ride."

He nodded. I got out of the truck and went to the back. I looked around: the sky was gorgeous. Dusk. The air was sweet. Smoke from Saskatchewan wildfires made the sun pink, and I loved the smell of a bushfire miles and miles away. I grabbed the Glad garbage bags holding the hindquarters of caribou.

"*Mahsi*," I said. He waved and I watched him drive away. Big Bingo tonight. He and Ehtsi would be playing hard. Standing with two huge hindquarters of caribou wrapped in four black Glad garbage bags, I wore my Chief Jimmy Bruneau long sleeve under my AFI hoodie and black jeans, fresh out of the dryer. My eyes stung I was so beat. Ehtse had told me that there was a grizzly banging on windows for the past three nights in Wha Ti. It was pregnant. The community tried chasing it away, even firing past her ears, but she's been coming back the past three nights banging on the windows and houses before being chased away by trucks and dogs. She's pregnant. What is she doing?

I'd been having bad dreams. Wicked, unholy dreams that had me yelling in my sleep. Last night I had the dream again of a child with its back to me in a field. I heard calls from the bush from animals I did not know. The child was wrapped in rags of hide and it had rotting meat for skin. Its hand held a leash of caribou sinew that held a weasel with a snapped neck. The weasel was rotten, a carcass. In this dream a raven was flying home. The child let out a whistle—a call? The raven was pulled from the air towards the child. The raven flapped wildly, but it was pulled towards the child who grabbed it with the force of its call. It then reached out and grabbed the wings and dug into the bird's body. The raven let out a cry that I would expect from a rabbit in a snare. I heard its wings snap under its skin as the flesh of the raven was dug into around the throat. This child then began to twist and peel the skin off the raven as it hissed, crying in terror and agony before I woke up. I could still hear the feathers snapping. The dreams have only gotten worse over the summer, and I'm just tired all the time now.

They can remember faces.... Something about the tar sands. Something about the end of the world. I'm sixteen. Why are these dreams so real?

Kids were playing across the street in the playground. Good for them. They were giving 'er on the monkey bars and on the swings.

This was the second time I was invited to Rupert's in my entire life so it was going to be interesting. The last time I was at the Spruces', my cousin Francis got all snaked up and got Indian Drunk so all the Dogribs got kicked out. But I guess all was forgiven now that Rupert's parents were out of town and he wanted to party. I wasn't a drinker. I was going there for Severina and a Coke. I just had to see her and find out where's she'd been this past week.

I had a crush on her. And to my surprise, it looked like she had a crush on me. The things we'd been doing all summer.... I was starving for her.

Rupert had called me this morning and asked that I bring as much meat as I could. We had lots so I wasn't worried, but it was strange how he told me to bring *ekwo*. It was like he ordered me, but that was fine with me: this was my key to getting to see Severina who hadn't returned my phone calls for days. She had my AFI CD and, if we weren't going to fool around anymore, I wanted it back—with the memories. Maybe our two weeks together meant nothing to her, but it meant everything to me. She was beautiful, and I wanted to be with her again.

The last night we hung out, she said she and her mom were driving from Behchoko to Yellowknife and they saw what looked like six horses running along the highway. As they got closer, they saw it was six moose running, galloping together, away from something. *Why?* I finally got to the front steps of the Spruce residence and—*Whoah!*—what was that smell?

The Spruce house was a fortress when you entered from the ground level. No windows. One door. Rupert's dad was the principal, and they were rich. They had the biggest house in town. As Rupert opened the door, I was met with a wave of flies that buzzed past me. This was strange.

"Is that all you brought?" Rupert peeked out of the door. His eyes were scared. What? This was lots. How many people were we feeding? His face was pale, long with worry. As he opened the door to let me in, the rankness was even stronger as it hit me in a hot wave: *Eeh mah!* It smelled like curdled milk and fish blood cooked together. As I walked into the house it became stronger: salt, blood, and a rotting of what—*meat and old batteries?*

"Keep your shoes on," Rupert said. "You can get more, right?" He leaned against the wall and started panting. He was sweating. It looked like he'd been crying.

"Yeah." *Where was the party?*

Richard Van Camp

"Okay," he took a big breath. "Okay."

"What's wrong?" I asked.

He motioned for me to follow and then he whispered, "Severina said you'd help us."

Severina? She said that? She said I'd help? Help what?

The stench kept getting stronger as I moved towards the bar and living room. It was hot, loud in my nose. My eyes started to water and I immediately switched to breathing through my mouth. I gagged as my eyes watered. The stench was so thick, I could pick it up with my mouth and tongue. The first time I was here I was blown away by how rich his family was: a huge flat screen TV, stacks of videos and DVDs all in their own libraries. Hundreds of movies. But, tonight, I looked down in astonishment. Hundreds of CDs and DVDs were out of their cases on the floor. A mirror was smashed in the hallway and glass was everywhere. Holes were punched in the wall—kicked, it looked like.

This was crazy, all this damage. What had happened? I knew Rupert's folks were away for a week but this was brutal. Tonight was supposed to be the party. Rupert's parents had a bar in the basement with mirrors everywhere so you could always see what was happening throughout the room. Norman walked into the bathroom and shut the door behind him without even looking at me. He looked horrible, defeated. There was a huge fish tank to the right. It took up half the wall, and yet the fish were all gone.

Rupert walked past me and touched my shoulder. "Put the meat in the freezer." There was a large white freezer in the hall and I opened the door. I opened it and it was completely empty except for a few black Glad garbage bags that were torn open.

Then I saw them in the far corner on the karaoke stage: the triplets, Marnie, Lisa and Shari, sitting on their own couch, all dressed the same. Their faces were grey, their eyes closed. They looked scared. They were all holding hands. They were squeezing each other's hands so tightly their arms were shaking. Then I heard them as their mouths moved in sync. They were praying. What the hell was going on here?

Across from them sat Dean Meddows, the town bully. *He has changed*, I thought. His mouth was open and he was panting, drooling all over himself. His shirt was soaked in it. The meat on his face looked like it was falling off. Blue veins bulged from around his lips and mouth. What was wrong with him? Dean sat on a chair facing the sisters, staring them down. I did not know if he even registered that I was there. He looked ten years older and his face was pale, covered in scabs. It looked like he'd smeared blood into his hair. He was also taller. Somehow, he was taller. Taller than me now. But thin. Too thin. He had scrape burns around his arms and wrists. *Rope?* I saw ropes that looked sawed through on the floor, around where he sat, the same with bungee cords that looked chewed through. Bottles were everywhere: vodka, gin, Jack Daniels. They were all empty. My heart sank and beat faster, colder. Fear sweat flashed in my armpits.

Rupert moved behind the bar. Petrified. Flies buzzed the air. He came back reading my eyes to see if I understood what was happening here. "What are you drinking?" he was asking but he was saying it different. He was saying it to act normal and buy time. I had to play along and find out all I could before I would know what to do. My eyes started to water with the stench I'd walked into. "Coke."

"Coke," he repeated and called to Tony. "Do we have any Coke?"

Tony looked at me and nodded and went down the back hall. He was scared, too. They stole glances at the girls, the triplets. Their look told me that they had lost control of everything here. The air around us was rotting. *Where was it coming from?* I looked around. There was a bucket in the middle of the floor with a piece of plywood over it in between the triplets and Dean, who was fixated on them. Fear prickled my skin all over. What would my Sensei do?

Tony returned with a six-pack of Coke cans, which he handed to Rupert. He buried his face under the collar of his shirt and took a big breath before coming up for air. Rupert had a huge A&W mug filled with ice waiting and poured to the top with a whole can. He motioned for me to sit at the bar. "Let's talk."

I could spy on everyone by using the mirrors if I stood right here. The triplets were to my right. I could hear them praying. It was "Hail Mary." What the hell was wrong with Dean?

"Is Snowbird in town?" Rupert asked. Snowbird was a medicine man who sometimes came to visit my family.

"Yeah." Snowbird had come over the other night. He was blind and had given me and my grandparents some rat root. Where was Severina? I looked at all the booze they had and it was safe to say they had everything, but the bottles were all empty. All of them. All of the bottles had their necks snapped off and broken.

Rupert's folks had an air hockey table. There were pictures of what looked like Mexico or Hawaii all over the walls. Rupert picked up a TV remote and turned it up a bit. I glanced at the mirrors. The triplets faced straight ahead but their eyes were still closed. I don't think they knew I was there. They needed to get out. Tony kept glancing our way. There was another wave of hot stink.

Rupert winked at me, trying to signal something I was supposed to understand before nodding towards the triplets. He then looked back at me. "Are you ready to join us?"

"What's going on?" I asked, acting interested, ready for anything.

Norman emerged from the bathroom. He was holding a large plastic Edmonton Oilers cup filled with something that made him gag. He looked at the triplets, then at Rupert. Norman had the sorriest eyes. Rupert nodded. "Help us," he whispered before spitting into the cup.

Rupert waved him away. "Hey. We're chatting."

Norman nodded. "Okay. Okay." He left, walking carefully, with his cup. He walked slowly to where the triplets were and knelt before Dean as if he were kneeling in church. Dean sniffed the air and nodded. Norman lifted the plywood over the bucket and poured the contents into the bucket. Flies crawled on the walls and floor and Dean appeared drunk. The triplets looked even more terrified than before.

Norman then replaced the plywood, rose carefully to stay away from Dean and walked back to us looking down.

"Can you get Snowbird?" Rupert asked. "Like, could you bring him here?"

I cleared my throat and thought about it. He was stalling for time, I could tell. I didn't want Snowbird here. He was blind, old.

I glanced in the mirror. It looked like one of the triplets was starting to cry. The other two said something quickly as if to warn her. Dean leaned closer towards them and I saw his throat start to move. I glanced at what Rupert had scribbled. *It's keeping everyone hostage.* Rupert wrote: *we have to distract it and run.* SAVE US PLEASE! IT IS EVIL!

It was like spider eggs burst under my skin and thousands of babies were making their way through me. I questioned him with my eyes and I answered back: *What? How can I help?*

He wrote: *I don't mean anything I'm saying. Severina's gone for help. She said for you to stall for time.* He wrote: *Don't let it make the sound.*

Stall for time? I didn't understand. I stood. "You said Severina was going to DJ tonight."

That's when he took my arm. "Don't—" I looked at him. His shirt was soaked in sweat. "Don't go," he urged. He wrote something else: *Dean has something inside of him we have to keep feeding.*

I read it and nodded before acting pissed off. "So when does this party start?"

Rupert wrote: *We have to get away.* He gave me a look that said we had to keep talking, that what was inside Dean was listening. Rupert scribbled furiously: *We can't let it outside.*

He nodded before announcing, "We have a gift for you." He turned on the TV. It was footage of Saddam Hussein being led to where he was about to be hanged. "He likes this. Do you think it was an accident that they released footage of Saddam Hussein being hung?"

Dean gave a throat grunt and turned to watch the screen. It was like he was blind and couldn't see me. He reached into the bucket and pulled a fistful of meat, blood, and maggots to feed from. Flies burst from the bucket and crawled in his hair before flying around the room. Dean licked all that he held and buried his face in it before eating some, smearing blood all over his jaw and then into his hair. His eyelids fluttered in delight and he made a guttural sound, like he opened his entire throat to receive the slop. I could hear chambers in his throat open as he let out a hot, throaty burp, vomiting everything back into his mouth to chew and chomp it up one more time before swallowing it again. He used his wrist and forearm to wipe most of it away.

My stomach rolled as I tried not to gag. The skin on my back lifted in fear and my legs felt weak. I glanced at the screen. Saddam looked scared, like a little boy. Men in black balaclavas and long trench coats surrounded him and led him towards where he was to be hung by a long yellow rope. My stomach began to roll. One man explained Saddam's execution to him. He was walking Saddam through what would happen to his throat and neck. Saddam looked around, all business, but deep down I could feel how terrified he was.

Dean vomited everything back into his mouth so he could chew it one more time before swallowing again. It was like he had molars in his throat that could grind it all over again. He grinned. His lower teeth were thick and jagged with points. He started moving his lower jaw back and forth, as if he could saw through bone if given a finger or limb.

What's inside of him? I wrote.

Rupert wrote quickly: *I don't know but it's getting stronger. Meat and blood calm it.*

I wrote: *Is it still Dean?*

He shook his head: *I don't know. I'm sorry. I caused this. We caused this by praying. Severina's getting help.*

Rupert's chin started to quiver. "They say this footage was leaked. But we all know it was to show the world the ultimate victory over him."

Dean gave a grunt from his chest and spun his head in my direction and began sniffing the air. He looked sick. His face was all boned out. One eye was black, the other bloodshot. Both eyes focused and unfocused on me. He started to shake. He then let out a long call, a growing, deep wail like a big cat, and my face tightened in fear. I became dizzy. I felt my strength—from the inside out—dissolve within me. His shoulders started to shake, and he began to breathe through his teeth while looking at me: "Huff huff huff." I felt like I was falling inside and steadied myself against the bar. Rupert produced a remote and spoke loudly. "We got *Faces of Death* and war footage. He likes it."

All of this was to keep its focus off of us. *Stall for time. Stall.* "Yes," I said. "Let's watch it."

Dean twisted his head to watch as if I was no longer on his radar. He liked this. As long as we went along with what it wanted, we were safe—for now. I started to feel my strength returning. Chase a wolf with a skidoo until its heart bursts—that's what this felt like, and I was the wolf. I let my breath out and refocused. That sound was how it claimed people. Its cry paralyzed. Its cry was a weapon. The screen was now a barrage of imagery: grainy footage of soldiers being blown apart or shot in wars from all over the world.

I started to undo my belt under the table. My Tlicho Power belt and buckle would be the weapon to attack and keep it away. Never mind stalling for time, I had to get these girls out of here. We all had to get out of here. I could see Norman and Tony, terrified, but looking at Rupert and me for direction.

Think, I thought. *Think this through. Think all of this through.*

Rupert scribbled: *Can you help me get everyone out?*

So it was claiming space through its growing strength and that sound. I couldn't let it make that sound. Dean started chuckling, watching all this footage. He started laughing and I could see his black gums, his jagged teeth. Wolverine teeth for crushing and pulling. He lifted the plywood off the bucket and scooped out another handful of maggots and blood soup, slurping it in his mouth, spilling more rot stink and flies into the air.

I nodded my head to his request. How could we get to the triplets? *Focus,* I thought. I felt cold seep into me. Sensei would tell me to think and focus.

Dean quit eating and tilted his head to listen to us.

I curled my hands into fists and prayed: "Creator, please help us. Whatever this thing is — it's too strong for just me. We need your mercy here for all of us. *Mahsi. Mahsi.* Please help us."

Rupert shook his head at me to indicate that he didn't mean what he was about to say as he raised his voice so Dean could hear: "He has a brother and a sister wishing to rise." Dean let out a low rasp to indicate he was pleased with this. He then let out a "glut" sound from his throat as if he was regurgitating the broth of what he'd been chewing. Rupert nodded with worry towards the triplets.

I glanced at the TV. My stomach started to roll when a soldier stepped on another soldier's skull and produced a knife while the downed soldier started to beg. I looked away, winced. Dean started cackling from deep within his chest and he picked up a bottle of Captain Morgan, and stuck the whole bottle in his mouth. He wrapped his lips around the bottle, clenched his teeth around the neck and tilted back. He started to drain the bottle in throaty gulps before chewing on the glass. He dropped the bottle when it was done and he kicked it away. He started panting again, looking at the triplets. They were crying now, holding hands and crying. Froth started to bubble out of Dean's mouth all over his shirt. *Wait,* I thought. *This is rabies. I read about this.*

Rupert closed his eyes as he spoke: "He said he will spare the girls if we bring him someone else. He wants a man. Snowbird."

Dean let out another wet rolling burp and rolled his eyes in delight. *The medicine man? Oh God.* What if it wasn't rabies? What if this was real? I wanted to run. I wanted to run and never stop. I wanted to run all the way back to Yellowknife and forget my life here, but I knew I had to protect everyone. I couldn't run. I had to get everyone to safety. I forced myself to grin: "That sounds great."

Dean made a sound, a groan of pleasure. He vomited back into his mouth and continued to chew. He burped and filled his cheeks with what he'd been eating before swallowing it all back down.

Rupert nodded, writing something down. *We have to get the girls out before the movie ends. We have two minutes left.* "He wants you to know something," he motioned for Tony and Norman to get the triplets away from Dean. Tony and Norman looked worried. *How?* they asked. "He promises to serve us if we bring him Snowbird. So join us now and serve. He will know not to hunt you if you serve him now."

Dean grunted his approval. He was hypnotized by the slaughter on the screen but he was still listening. He moved his jaw back and forth and I could hear his massive molars and teeth in his jaw scraping over each other like rocks. *It can sharpen its own teeth!*

What spirit—what monster was this? My stomach rolled with fear. *What would Conan do?* I thought. He'd play along to find out more information. I was cold inside and shivering. "This is awesome," I bluffed. "I'm honoured you've called me here. I can bring you the medicine man called Snowbird. He is blind and trusts me. Tell me more."

Rupert motioned for Tony and Norman to hurry but they were too scared. They shook their heads. "To rise, they need the old man." Rupert made a motion that it was up to us to get the triplets.

I nodded and moved my hands to my belt under the table. "I can trick the old man," I said. "He is weak."

Rupert fake-smiled and started to move from behind the bar. He motioned for us to move towards Dean. I nodded, moving slowly. I unhooked my belt, pulling it out so it would fall by my leg without Dean seeing. "Once he has the old man, the mother can give birth to more of them. Her son has asked you to join us in their killing return," Rupert said.

My mouth dropped. *Mother? Killing return? What?*

Dean hummed from his chest in approval and reached for more slop from the bucket. He worked his jaw again and we could all hear his teeth like bone on bone, molars against fangs. Those little hands of his were no longer little. They were long fingered, thick knuckled and strong. With claws that looked like they belonged on a grizzly.

"His mother is gaining in power," Rupert announced with a grimace.

Dean nodded twice. He grunted to indicate he was listening as he watched the horrific footage of war and killing. "Bear," Rupert said to me, "her son is honouring you tonight by asking you to be here. Bring us Snowbird and you can join us."

The footage ended. Dean stopped smacking his lips and grinding his teeth. He looked confused, blinked twice, realized the movie was over and then looked at us. I quit moving, my hand squeezing my belt so I could use it as a weapon.

Dean looked at Rupert and Norman before gripping his seat and rising slowly, claiming its space. Dean had grown. He was now taller than all of us. His arms did not fit his body. They were too long. His hands were so long they looked like feet. He began to look at us and shake. Tony and Norman glanced at me for direction. They also readied their hands to cover their ears. That was when Dean spoke, looking down at us. His body started shaking. "Will the cunt mouth bring us Smoke Eyes?"

Rupert lowered his head and looked down as if not to invite an attack. "He said he is honoured. He will bring you the enemy magician."

As the triplets held hands, prayed and wept together on the couch behind him, Dean Meddows lowered his voice and started panting. He looked at me once, directly into my eyes. God, his eyes were cold. They were the eyes of something dead staring at me. I pretended to fawn and got ready to strike with my belt. *Aim for the nose*, I thought.

"Bear is honoured to serve you," Rupert called to Dean.

No, I thought. *Don't say my name. It must not know my name.*

Rupert spoke. "He has brought you two hindquarters of caribou as a gift."

Tony agreed. "Bear will help us."

Dean's eyes started to darken, his left eye dilated. "He's lying." His lips started to tremble as I heard a mewling inside of him—a rising growl in his chest. He raised his arms to his sides and hissed like a large cat. My strength left me as I saw his eyes change. All I saw in them was hate and cruelty, starvation. *Not human*, I thought. *He's not human anymore. Wait—they're all wrong. It is just rabies—*

The sound hit me before I heard it. The tiny bones in my ear lobes suddenly became rattling knives and my tongue twisted backwards with the force of his scream. I felt like I'd been shot through the spine. Time slowed and everyone in the room covered their ears. As much as I wanted to, I'd need both hands for what I had to do. I readied my belt. The wrap-around muscles in Dean's face started to stretch and ripple under his skin. His mewling grew and it hit me like a

winding cold drill through my skull don't faint don't weaken

Dean started moving his jaw back and forth, unhinging it. He started to hiss and jerk towards me. He started to grow in the arms, neck, legs. I saw the skin of his face shake as he started to call something behind him forward.

Don't, I thought.

Don't let it make that sound. Fight the fear. Break it—

We could hear popping underneath his skin as ligaments and sinew stretched beyond their capacity. Dean's cry hit me in the chest—I could feel it—and I felt the hair on my arms prickle in fear. It was like someone poured ice water all over me. I felt the strength leave my legs in cold fear.

But he was only inhaling.
My arms dropped
to my sides
the more Dean made this mewling cry

Richard Van Camp

all I want to do
is let go,
fall into the dizzying grip
of this call.
My blood starts to thin,
my heart squeezes itself to stillness.
I can't feel my hands
I can't feel them.
I feel skinless.
It's trying to break my mind.

I was just about to sink to the floor in surrender, about ready to drop my belt to the floor when a chair exploded over Dean's head. Dean raised his arm and looked at Tony, breaking his cry. Tony stood there holding the broken legs of the chair. Dean backhanded him, throwing him back. Dean started to shake uncontrollably.

"Bear!" one of the triplets called. "Help us—please! Dean's a windigo!"

I used the moment of confusion to raise my fist with my belt, plant my feet on the floor and strike Dean in the mouth. I had to stop him from making that sound. Dean's eyes were full black now, eyes of pure hate, pure ferocity. I wound up and whipped him again, striking his nose. Blood began to flow.

"You girls!" I yelled. "Get up and get out of here. Run!"

I wound up again. The triplets—their eyes wide with fear—looked at Dean and started screaming. *Now*, I thought. *Now!*

Be brave, I thought. *Be brave for them. Buy time and do not show fear.* Whatever Dean was, he would taste the bite of Tlicho power! I wound up and started whipping his face with my buckle as the muscles in Dean's face popped as his jaw unhooked itself from under his skin. I heard cartilage and muscle ripping inside his neck. His eyes rolled back as he started his cry again. I weakened but fought this power. I felt the ground move under my feet. It was like the whole house was moving, like a tornado was being born inside him. Dean was growing. His back hunched. I gripped my belt and backed up. I had to stall to get everyone out. Tony was still dazed and rolling around, trying to get up. Rupert grabbed the triplets and started pulling them past us. Norman started yelling, "We have to get outside. Run!"

Tony was still on his back and I had to stall for time. I would not back down. I had to break its focus from the rest of the group.

"Don't let it bite you!" Rupert yelled from the hallway.

Dean's body was still changing and he focused his attention on the belt, as if part of him remembered how I kicked his ass when he tried to steal it from me in Simmer. He stood lopsided. One of his eyes was monstrous and swollen. The other looked human. I could hear his tongue moving in his mouth as he took a large breath from his throat. I heard panting. "Help me, Bear," I heard him croak. "Something bit me." His eyes locked on mine before rolling back inside his skull. That was Dean's voice.

"Dean?" I asked.

From his throat he began that dizzying cry again. Dean's jaw now hung low and his teeth were sharp, like something canine for ripping. He pulled his bloody face up, into a grimace, so that his eyes sank back into his skull. He had become this creature that wanted to feed. He raised his arms up like wings and they started to grow. I looked up at the full size of him. His rib cage heaved under his skin to receive all he could eat.

Looking at the slop bucket that was beside him, I could smell that it fed on blood and meat. I remembered Sensei's training: *Defeat the weapon, defeat the opponent.* Its form was physical power, yes, but its design was wrong. Its jaw was larger than its head—like an old jackfish. This was the flaw. Its weakness was its greed for feeding.

Before Dean could grow in power or make the dizzying cry, I spun and whipped the belt, striking his face again and again. He swung one arm to block the lashings. Dean's jaw hung open and I saw his bottom teeth. They were brown with filth and his incisors jutted up and out like a bear's. His nose split where I hit him. He started lapping at the blood. Dean kept looking at the belt, trying to remember where he had seen it before.

Give it what it wants, I thought. *Buy time so everyone can get away.*

"You want blood?" I asked. "Here it is." I moved fast, kicking the slop bucket by our feet so blood, slime, maggots and meat sprayed his pants and shirt. My eyes watered from the stink and I started gagging. Dean spun his head and started sniffing himself. Muck spilled from his mouth as he started licking and lapping the air.

I looked to Tony. "Run," I said. "Get out!"

Tony rose and, from my left, he scrambled up and limped out behind me, whimpering at first and then screaming as he left. I could feel Rupert in the hallway watching us. "You too," I said, "Go! Run!"

He did. Rupert called, "Don't let it outside!" Everyone was safe now, except me.

Dean continued to lap and lick at his own clothes and skin. Fear rippled through me but I had to stall for time so everyone could get away. *Don't let this out of the house*, I thought. *Don't let this out into Behchoko.*

I got my belt ready and aimed for Dean's eyes. I thought of the kids playing outside across the street. *No way*, I thought. *You're not getting them.*

Sensei told me that to become a ninja, you had to die first, and this was my chance. If this was it, let it be defending my community. Either way, this beast would not get out of the house. I had the power of my ancestors and I had Sensei's training. I knew what I had to do.

Prepare, I could hear Sensei say. I shifted to Bear Stance and imagined a wall of concrete behind me. I would not be moved. The nine points of contact on each foot reached the centre of the earth. I knew I had to hold this ground until Severina returned, but I was already a ghost fighting for a body. My spirit was strong. I could think through the fear. I could. I used the time as it feasted to breathe, center myself and ready myself for the next attack. If death was soon, let it be. Let my name live on as someone who saved others.

Dean's face contorted and pulled itself outwards, drawing its nose inward to transform into something with the rotting face of a dog or wolf. I realized my belt was wrapped around my fist so tight my fingers were purple. My blood turned to slush. "Jesus Christ," I yelled. "What the fuck are you?"

I went to go whip him in the skull but he slapped my belt buckle away. He lunged towards me, biting towards my stomach when I heard something snap like a whip. It leapt backward, screaming in agony. The thing—whatever this was—backed up to examine the damage. It looked down. Its fingers started to twist into themselves up and backwards. It howled in pain..

"What is your weapon?" it asked. *Me? What did I have?*

The beast of Dean pointed his mangled hand at my hoodie. "Give."

He charged me again and I whipped him in the mouth. His head snapped back and a tooth—an incisor as big as my thumb—fell out of his mouth onto the floor.

It looked at his hands again. They were broken in half, split and exposing meat. Blood started to seep over his own wounds. With this, the demon grinned, closed its eyes slowly and started slurping, feeding on its own hands, lapping up the blood that spurted up and out. It sounded like ice cracking under his skin. He howled in agony but could not stop feeding.

"Sorry," it growled, with blood on his teeth. He flicked his tongue across them. "Tell… m-mm… mom I'm sorry." His eyes rolled in their sockets towards me. "Bear."

"Grab the tooth," a voice said in my right ear. "I will help you. *But you need that tooth.*" Panic. *Shit.* How could I do this?

I carefully knelt and plucked the tooth up before walking backwards, backing my way out of the main room and down the hallway. I put it up my sleeve. I had to save Dean, whatever was left of him inside that thing.

The caribou meat! This could buy us time.

As it began to eat its own fingers Dean screamed in hysterical pain, as if what was left of him knew what was happening but the beast inside him could not stop itself. I turned and I ran, almost slipping on the CDs and DVDs on the floor. I raced to the freezer and grabbed the hindquarters and brought them out to show Dean.

He looked at the meat as I unwrapped it.

"Feast on this," I said. I rolled the frozen meat towards it on the floor and Dean hunched to begin ripping into it. Its mouth opened to feast and rip and shred. I then rolled the other hindquarter towards it. *There.* Dean would be safe as long as it could eat.

This was a lot of meat. Dean would be safe for a little while. He held his broken hands up and away from his body as it fed.

"Dean," I said. "What is left of you, I'm trying to save. Can you tell me what hurts you?"

With his eyes closed, I could hear Dean humming as he swallowed. He arched his neck back to swallow a huge chunk of meat. I spoke. "I will give you my belt, the one you tried taking from me. I'll give it to you, okay, but you have to help me save you. What hurts you?"

Dean listened as the beast he was becoming was soothed—as long as it was eating. He let out a loud and wet "glut" as he swallowed.

"Water," he spoke. "It hurts it if there's loud water."

"Okay," I said. "I'm going to call for help. Keep eating the meat and we'll get you help, okay?"

All of a sudden, the door opened a bit. "Bear?" a voice called. I turned slowly, positioning myself between Dean and the voice.

And who did I see but Severina standing with wide eyes behind two men: Snowbird and Torchy. Their faces were warlike, ready for anything. Around their heads and throats were bands of yarrow braided together. In Torchy's hands were spears and clubs of antlers.

Torchy spoke quickly. "Severina, go with him."

Severina? Severina looked at me and nodded. She was dressed in black, her hair in a ponytail. She looked strong. Ready for anything.

"Wait," Snowbird said. "Do you have the rat root?"

I stopped. "Rat root?"

He pointed to my jacket. "Did he ask you for it?"

I looked down and reached inside. I was shaking and felt it. I pulled it out and there it was: the rat root he'd given me when he'd come over for supper. It had the red string on it. This is what broke Dean's hands. It was protection! "Yes. It asked for it."

"Burn it now. Remember," Snowbird said, "we must save Dean. Do you have the tooth?"

I reached in my sleeve, surprised. "Yes."

"Give," he held his hand out and I handed it to him.

"Do you want me to get the priest?" Severina asked.

"*In le.*" Snowbird shook his head. "These are older than Jesus."

Snowbird nodded and placed his hands on Torchy's shoulder. He carried a large moosehide bag filled with something that smelled strong. Yarrow? Bear grease? That was when I noticed all of them had yarrow stalks tied around their arms and legs. I could smell the plant, and it cleared the stench from my nose right away with its sweetness. Torchy placed himself first and opened the door to face what was inside. In his left hand he had a spear. In his right, he held an axe.

"No," I winced. "Whatever that is, Dean's still inside it. I heard his voice. It's feeding on two frozen caribou hindquarters right now so it's distracted."

I watched Torchy's hands. They clenched and unclenched. His sleeves were rolled up and I saw a tattoo of scars across his right fore-arm. He was looking forward to fighting this.

"I swear to you that Dean's still inside whatever that is," I said. "He told me whatever he's becoming hates the sound of loud water."

Torchy only looked at me once. His eyes were on fire. I saw them register. He released his axe to me. "Whatever it asked for," he said, "burn it."

"It asked for Snowbird," I said.

Snowbird looked at me once quickly, with milky eyes. He nodded. "Be my eyes," he said to Torchy as he put his head down. He started chanting. He was praying in Tlicho. He opened the door. "I see a tall man eating meat about thirty steps ahead," Torchy said. "He's ripping into it with his teeth. His hands look broken."

Snowbird produced a small stone, an amulet of bone, and a braid of hair. He then started to chant. In his other hand he held a sandwich bag packed with red meat. I smelled something like rotten eggs. *Sulfur?*

"Turn on the taps," I said. "They hate the sound of running water." Torchy narrowed his eyes and focused. He was chewing something slowly. Rat root?

Snowbird was focused, too. The blind holy man placed his left hand on Torchy's shoulder and they moved as one into the house. "Close the door behind me. Severina, turn on the taps."

Severina did as she was told. She gagged when she caught a whiff of the house. I immediately heard water run from the tub inside the bathroom. I heard a whimper begin from inside the house from the screened window in the bathroom. Then it turned to shrieking. What was inside Dean was terrified. I looked at the playground. All the kids were gone. Thank God.

"Let's go," Severina said. "We have to go." She took my hand and we ran as fast as we could together to the residence.

We ran. We ran through town without speaking. I had the axe. We ran and I asked her only once. "Tell me about the rat root," I said.

"I don't know. But we must burn it. Anything it asked you for—whatever they ask for, you must burn."

They? There were more. "What was that? What was inside Dean?"

"A Wheetago," she whispered.

"Wheetago?" I repeated.

"Shh," she said. "They're listening." My skin tightened in fear again. I held onto Torchy's axe, ready to draw it if anything came at us.

We ran past CJBS to her house. It was still light out. There was a burn barrel in the backyard. I placed the axe on a picnic table on its side, keeping it close.

There was a box of matches, kindling, old branches ready to go. I lit a match and touched it to old newspaper, last week's *News/North*. Sparks rose as the fire engulfed the twigs and newspaper I had set inside there earlier. Thank God it hadn't rained.

"Hurry," she said. I could see her ankles and wrists had yarrow tied around them as well.

I pulled out Snowbird's rat root. "This is the only thing that saved me," I said. "That and my belt." The rat root—this was why it couldn't come close. This is why its bones shattered and split when it came for me.

I was scared. I was scared that the world would know now about what I had seen. I took the rat root with the red string. I did not understand why we had to burn it but that thing had asked for it. It had protected me. Snowbird had given it to me two nights ago when he'd come over for supper. "I have a gift," he'd said. "Keep it with you." He patted my hoodie pocket. "*Na.* Here."

That was all he said. *He must have known.* I dropped the rat root into the fire. We watched it go up. It curled and bubbled as the flames caught it.

"I don't understand," I said. "How did it get here?"

"Bad medicine," Severina said, making the sign of the cross. "It's all bad medicine. Those kids were praying for power and it came to them as a coyote. It spoke to them and bit Dean."

I stopped. "That's a coyote inside of Dean?"

"A Wheetago," she repeated softly.

"A what?"

"Those who suffer. He wanted you to bring him Snowbird?"

I nodded.

"Oh thank God you got everyone away," she said. "Thank God. Thank God."

She started to shake. "Evil," she spoke. "It's all evil."

"Tell me about these...." I asked. "How do you say it?"

She looked at me. "You don't know?"

I shook my head. "I've heard of the Bushmen and the little people but not these."

She took a big breath and watched the fire. "The Wheetagos are cannibals. They're from the south but the people there are strong. Their medicine and Wheetago hunters have pushed them north. These... things, the more they eat the hungrier they become; the more they drink the thirstier they become. Maybe they got bit or cursed. But they suffer. If they don't eat, they will chew on their tongues and lips, gnaw on the insides of their cheeks, bite their own fingers off at the joints and suck on them just to feed."

I dry swallowed. *This was my dream. Last night. The tar sands. The Shark Throats. It was all coming true!* I nodded, wincing at what I saw in Dean. "Can they save him?"

"They'll have to blind him."

Blind him? I thought of Torchy's spear.

I got scared to hear this and wished I had my belt. It was still there. We had the axe. Northern lights washed in greens and blues across the sky. Silent. Ancient. Could God protect us from this? If these were older than Jesus, I bet they used the northern lights to hunt under.

Severina threw branches and kindling on the flames. "If you bring them what they ask for they can give birth to their own family." I closed my eyes as this washed over me. I thought of the bucket that it spat into.

"How do you know all this?" I asked.

"Snowbird is my adopted grandfather. He is a Wheetago hunter. We've been preparing with Torchy and the triplets."

"The triplets?" I said. "They were part of this?"

"Yes, they were to stall for time."

"They could have been bitten."

"No," she said. "They were protected."

She held up rat root. "Snowbird gave seven of us medicine."

My jaw dropped. "This was all part of a plan."

"Snowbird saw all of this in a dream. He planned tonight out. We were to bait the Wheetago and you were to save us."

I just about fainted. "No… but you left."

"Yes, my job was to get Snowbird when you arrived. He knew you'd stand up to it. He saw all of this in his dream."

"But"—I paused—"Snowbird is blind."

"He wasn't always," she said and put her rat root into her pocket.

Not born blind? Was he a Wheetago once?

"He wants to train you for more."

I froze. "More what?"

She nodded. "He told me you have medicine and we will need it."

The voice! A voice spoke to me. Telling me about the tooth.

"Medicine? Take it easy."

"We cannot let them give birth to more."

My blood ran cold. I thought of the tooth I knocked out of Dean's mouth, the eyetooth. Could this be used as a weapon against them? I thought again of what Snowbird said, how they were older than Jesus. If so, this would mean they'd been beaten and there were techniques to fight and kill them. But were there techniques to save the people inside them? Dean was still in there. They had to save him. What did the dream say: *stop the Tar Sands—at all costs.*

"Thank God you're okay," Severina said. "You got the triplets out. You got Rupert and his friends out."

I sighed. My arms were rubbery and I was exhausted. It saw me. Its eye flashed hate and hunger and ferocity. "How does it give birth?"

She thought about it and spoke quietly. She started to shake. "From their mouths."

"Jesus Christ," I said. So it was true. The dream was unfolding through all of us.

Severina leaned into me, hugging me. "Thank you for saving my cousins," she whispered and kissed my neck. Her lips were cold. "There better be a fuckin' heaven after all this." *Do something,* I thought. Focus and do something. *This is your chance.* I held her. I held her by the fire. I had never been hugged like this before. I closed my eyes and hugged her back. I licked my split lip before kissing her gently. She kissed me back. She was shivering.

We heard the sirens of the police, the ambulance and then the fire truck going towards the part of town where Rupert lived. Then we heard the dogs start to howl. I did not know what to think anymore, except that Snowbird and Torchy would come back after dealing with whatever it was in Dean. I looked at Severina and she hugged me again. We were the perfect size for each other. I looked up and the northern lights weaved their way over us, braiding themselves into blues and a night rainbow of blues and greens.

The howling of the dogs was met with a new sound, a yipping and crazy cry of coyotes. Coyotes. Yes, it was true. They'd moved up here two winters ago and we could hear them at night. They too were not from here. Nor did they belong here. But they were. Their yips and snapping barks rose in a chorus that drove the dogs crazy. Were they the scouts for these Dog Men? It was like the whole town was howling now as I tightened my hug on Severina. This war was just beginning. They had risen and I had the training of my Sensei. I held Severina close. With Snowbird, Torchy and her by my side, we could face them. They were using dog medicine. Sulfur in the meat to defeat the spirit inside, maybe. This was dog medicine I had learned from my ehtsi.

If they can give birth, they need each other. "It's going to be okay," I said, eyeing the axe on the table. I closed my eyes and kissed the top of her head, inhaling Severina's scent and the yarrow ties around her. "I promise."

To my surprise, Severina whispered in my ear. "Snowbird has a message for you."

I leaned back. "What?"

She leaned into me and pulled me close. "He said, 'If you save everyone and put yourself before the beast and walk away, then you will know how heroes are born.'" And there I was, anointed finally as the warrior I'd always wanted to be.

Tonight we would wait to see what would happen to Dean. Then I would talk to Snowbird. The dream said it was sent to two people. After, we'd have to decide what to do about the tar sands. We had to stop them. We had to.

That grizzly, the pregnant mother, I realized. This is a mother slapping her hands against our windows with new life inside of her telling us that the murder of our world was coming. Those moose running away. *They were all trying to warn us:* things were going to get bloody and worse. I knew, as the cries of the dogs and the coyotes grew, that deep down inside this was not over. Not yet... no way....

Children of the Sundance

"LET'S PLAY A NEW GAME," TREYTON SAID.

I placed Skeletor at the head of my attack armada. "What kind of new game?" I was totally going to win Catapults tonight before the pizza party, before Treyton and Blaire would try to leave their bodies. My friends and their armies would not stand up to any of my Ninjalix tonight. I'd been practising with the catapult Brutus helped me make, and I could pretty much take out anything within a five-foot radius.

It was Friday night—the best night of the week. Another sleep over at Blaire's. This meant four handmade pizzas—three Hawaiian (my fave) and one with caribou meat (all for Mr. Sparrow)—and a two-litre of milk left in the freezer for exactly the perfect moment it became the sweet slush of snowflakes. And you could eat and drink as much as you wanted. That was the best part. Not like Trey's whose folks were cheap.

"What are you planning now?" Blaire asked suspiciously.

Treyton sat back. "It's a new game that will help us."

You had to be careful with Treyton's new games. Since I was initiated, he was getting us to try to leave our bodies at night as we lay in our sleeping bags with all three of our heads touching. "Can you feel it?" he'd ask. "Can you?"

I'd try but I'd always fall asleep. Trey and Blaire said they flew together at night. I wanted to believe them. I wanted so badly to believe that I, too, could leave my body and float around town and see what Chandra, Marcy and Sharon were up to. I'd love to sit in their room and watch them do homework or get their clothes ready for the next day at school. In the mornings, Blaire and Trey would both talk about their adventures and I'd watch them closely to see if they were lying. Their stories were crazy. Lately, they both said they felt like we were being followed, like there was something behind them waiting above the house that wanted them to keep flying up and up, and they did because they were scared, but the higher they rose, they felt lighter and lighter until Treyton realized that if they flew one mile more their bodies would die.

Thank God I never went with them. I carried a small thumb knife my dad gave me since then. It fit into my pocket and was razor sharp. Treyton and Blaire quit trying for a few weeks, but I had a sense they wanted to "astral project" tonight.

"So do you?" Treyton asked. "Do you want to play a new game?"

I studied Treyton and realized he hadn't set up any of his G.I. Joes or any of his HISS Tanks. Destro and his buddies were all there, but they were still lying on their backs and their weapons were still in their baggies. Trey had some first generation G.I. Joes we weren't allowed to touch because the thumbs were delicate. His dad gave them to him and Trey made a point of reminding us of that every time we played Catapults.

"Trey," I asked. "What kind of new game?"

"Well," he said. "You know next year we're going to high school, right?"

Blaire and I looked at each other. "Yeah."

"It's time we helped each other. You know, build each other up?"

"How?" Blaire sat back.

Blaire's speech impediment was getting better. His r's were sometimes w's. It was like he was missing his top teeth. "Later" was "Ladew." "Never" was "nevew." I didn't mind it. We'd gotten used to it since kindergarten. I actually looked forward to it. It was kind of like my blankie.

"Well," Treyton said. "What if we played a game where two of us stayed in the room and the other one left and the two of us who stayed in the room got to talk about what we don't like about the other and then when we're ready, we knock and the other person comes back in and then we tell them about what they have to work on."

I felt my cheeks starting to burn. "Why do we have to do that? Why can't we just play Catapults and eat pizzas?"

"Because we need to get stronger, you know?"

I looked at Blaire. He was thinking about it.

"I don't like this." I checked my Transformers watch and realized supper wouldn't be ready for at least another forty minutes. Why did the Sparrows have to eat so late?

"Okay," Blaire said. "I think we should do this. I'll go fewst."

"What?" I asked. "Blaire?"

He shrugged. "You guys will probably talk about my speech impediment but that's okay. I'm... wherking on it." He stood up and walked out the door, closing it gently behind him.

I looked at Treyton. "This feels mean." I wasn't thinking so much about Blaire. I was worried about me. What if they said something that would wreck me forever? I was Dogrib. They were white. What if this became an issue again? I'd already ditched Brutus as a friend so I could be with Trey and Blaire, so there was no going back now.

"Clarence," he said. "We gotta. I think about how to get better all the time. Don't you?"

There was that tone again. It was the same tone he used the first time we had a sleep over and he asked if I had brought any jammies to Blaire's. "No," I said. I was going to use my long johns and Star Wars T-shirt. "Only Indians sleep in their clothes," he said and we all laughed, but that stung. It hurt. I thought of my parents and hoped he was kidding but, deep down, I knew he wasn't.

"Hey," I said, looking at my He-Man collection and my catapult. "I'm happy. Let's just have a pizza party and then you guys can try and leave your bodies later."

He shook his head. "Don't you want to grow?"

I sighed. "I don't want to be mean to Blaire."

"Blaire," he spat. "He's not even trying with that speech thing. He still talks baby talk. Don't you think that'll slow us down at the bush pawties?"

I couldn't believe he'd make fun of Blaire like that. I wanted to leave but Mom and Dad were at the drum dance. Plus it was snowing like crazy. Plus I saw the pizza doughs rising on the counter when I came in!

"Okay," he said. "We won't talk about his speech impediment, but look at his face. Look at those moles. They're spreading."

"What?" I said. "Where?"

He pointed to the right side of his face. "Around his jaw. There's seven of them. Last year he only had five." He then pointed out a map along his face, starting with his head and working down his entire face. "They look exactly like the Big Dipper now."

"Well what can he do about that?"

Treyton lowered his voice. "He could get them scraped off."

"What?"

"Or bleached. I asked my mom about it."

"This is dumb," I said. "You're being mean. First of all, Blaire's really trying with his speech therapist. Do you see him going every Wednesday? And he's in there for over an hour. He has cue cards and even his parents go with him."

"Not good enough," Treyton exhaled like he just had a smoke. "He'll slow us down."

"Slow *you* down," I wanted to say. This was happening more and more. It was like Treyton was biding his time at the pizza parties. He and I used to be so close. We used to walk around for hours down by the landslide, exploring, climbing, building. Blaire started tagging along and it turned out Blaire's parents were fun. Treyton's parents were cheapskates and never put on the heat when we slept over.

There was a knock on the door. It was Blaire. "Can I come back?"

I looked at Treyton and gave him a dirty look. "Yes."

Blaire walked in with his head down and he put his hands in his pockets. He had grey socks on with a hole in the big toe on one of them. I wanted to run up and hug him. "Clarence and I think you need to lose the baby talk," Treyton announced.

"I did not say that!" My ears started to burn.

"You did," Treyton said.

"It's okay," Blaire said. "Go on."

"Blaire," I said. "I didn't. I never—"

"We also think you need to do something about your moles."

Rather than look up and punch Treyton in the face, Blaire nodded slowly. "You're right. They're in the shape of the Big Dipper."

Wah! I thought. This is the worst pizza party ever!

"Blaire," I said. I was trying to blanket him in sorries and explanations, but he held a hand up and started talking. "I want to thank you guys. I am trying to talk better. See that? I said it. *Better.* I couldn't say that a year ago." He closed his eyes and put his hand over his chest and pressed down softly. "The new speech therapist says I just need to slow down."

Treyton and I look at each other. Blaire was speaking perfectly.

"It's just that...I get so excited about things...I sometimes forget to breathe and then...I make mistakes. I'm sorry if I embarrass you."

"No," I said and stood. "Blaire, you're my best friend. I swear I never got embarrassed."

He looked down and nodded.

I glared at Treyton. "This is dumb. I don't want to play this."

"Also," Blaire continued. "I agree with what you said about my moles. I wasn't born with them. They just keep happening. I can go see a doctor if you guys want."

"No," I said. "Just leave them. They're not doing anything." But I looked and Treyton was right: they did line up like the Big Dipper.

"I don't think it would hurt, Blaire," Treyton said. "You're doing great with your speech stuff. See? This is a great game. Ask them about bleaching."

My jaw dropped. I turned and was about to go after Treyton when Blaire spoke. "Okay," he said and sat down. He started rocking back and forth and pulled his favourite He-Man, Grizzlor, close to his chest. Grizzlor had fur all over his body so he was still like a teddy bear. "I needed to hear all of that. Thanks, guys. I want to be stronger for you—and in case that spirit comes back when we float."

I rubbed Blaire's shoulder and sat beside him. That only took up ten cheap minutes. Another thirty dumb minutes before supper. "I'll go next," Treyton said. "I'm ready. Be honest. I really need you guys to give it to me. We have to get into Roy Bartleman's parties. They're supposed to be awesome."

Who cared about Roy Bartleman's dumb parties? I shook my head and made a promise to not hold back. He shut the door behind him.

"Blaire," I said quickly. "I swear to God I never said anything bad about your speech—like how you talk."

He put his hand on my arm. "It's okay."

"But I need you to know that. You and I were altar boys. I swear on the Bishop's ring and holy catechism that I never said anything about you or your moles. You're one of my best friends." As I said that, I felt a shift. Something inside me. Yup. It had happened: Blaire was my new best friend. Treyton was pushed down one stair of friendship as Blaire took a step up. "In fact, you're my best friend as of right now. How about that?"

"Cool," he petted Grizzlor. "I believe you."

I let out the biggest sigh of relief ever. Maybe this night could be saved.

"Treyton needs to work on his parents," Blaire said. "They're mean."

I thought about it. "How?"

"When we go over there, they make us haul wood and shovel. They don't shovel all week and it's up to us to do their walks and two driveways. It's cheap."

"Yeah," I agreed. "And they never turn on the heat in their basement when we sleep over."

He nodded. "They suck."

Just the way he said it, I saw the little boy inside of him. "Yeah," I smiled. "They suck. They also never really talk to us like the way your folks do. They don't cook for us and all we get is Tang—that we have to mix—and a half-bag of Cheezies."

"Always," he said.

"Okay," I said. "That's good. Can we eat?"

"Should we tell him about the noises?" He looked up at me.

"What noises?"

"You know," Blaire said. "When he eats."

It didn't happen often but when Treyton drank he'd make these puppy noises, like when they're hungry, or when we ate something really hot. He'd make this noise like a runt puppy.

I sighed. "I don't know, Blaire. I don't think he knows he does that."

"But isn't this game about making us stronger?" He grinned. It was an ugly grin. A revenge grin. And it was reaching out to me to join in, like that spirit in the sky inviting them to fly up and up.

"Wait," I said and there was a knock on the door.

"Can I come in?" Treyton asked as he walked into the room.

"Yeah," Blaire said.

Treyton looked at both of us and he put his hands in his pocket. His socks were pure white. His jeans were ironed and his hair was perfect. He played hockey and was getting muscles. I had a sense that we'd lose him to the cool kids the second we walked into PWK. It would only be Blaire and me and our He-Man wars and pizza parties.

"What did you guys talk about?" Treyton looked directly at both of us. He was ready.

"You tell him," Blaire said to me.

I took a big breath. I didn't feel bad about his parents, but I wasn't so sure about the puppy noises. "Trey," I said and took a big breath, "Blaire and I both agree that your parents could try harder...with us."

"How'd you mean?"

"Well," I said. "They make us work hard when we go over there with shovelling and hauling wood."

"You guys don't even come over anymore," he said.

Blaire held up his hand to show we were still talking. "They also didn't turn on the heat when we slept over," I said.

"I hate my mom," Trey said coldly.

Blaire and I hissed when we heard it.

"What?"

"She's a pig. My dad totally bows down to her. I made up my mind today that I hate them both. I can't wait to leave this town."

"Trey," I said and made my way towards him but he stepped back.

"What else?" he asked. His cheeks flared red.

"Treyton," Blaire said. "We're sorry."

"No," he said. "What else?"

I looked to Blaire to ease off about the puppy noises.

"Clarence said you also make puppy noises when you eat," Blaire said quickly.

"What?" he said. "When?"

"Clarence said when you eat something you like or in gym when you down water."

"Take it easy," he said. "What do they sound like?"

Blaire looked at me. "Do your impression."

I burst out laughing out of shock. "I'm not…Blaire…I did not say…"

Blaire started laughing, too.

Treyton looked at us with puppy eyes. "Are you guys kidding me?"

"Yeah," Blaire said. "We were just kidding. You don't make puppy sounds."

Oh man! I let out another sigh. This was not the time to talk about it after what he said about his parents.

Blaire and Treyton both looked at me. "Okay, Clarence. Now it's your turn."

I looked at both of them and realized that this was it: this was my moment. I took a second to memorize them the way they were now and tonight. Treyton was getting muscles and Blaire was getting peach fuzz. I'd known them since kindergarten. Some grades I couldn't remember but I had all our class photos tacked to my wall. I looked at them every night before bed. I squinted out of my left eye to cover up Brutus, who always pushed everyone out of the way so he could stand right next to me.

"Go easy," I smirked but they weren't smiling. They were already thinking. They better not say anything about me being Indian. If they did, I'd never forgive them because of what I did to Brutus. I winced when I thought of how I'd betrayed him to be here.

I grimaced and took Beast Man with me. His whip was cheap so I always had He-Man's battle-axe as his weapon. I held him like a teddy bear and closed the door behind me. It was February—the coldest month in Smith—and the cement floor downstairs was freezing so I decided to walk upstairs. I could smell the pizzas in the oven and Mr. Sparrow was upstairs reading, listening to the radio. Country and Western was on and he was a huge reader of Westerns. I could smell the pizzas baking in the oven. My mouth started to water.

"Hi, Mr. Sparrow," I said.

He looked up and smiled. "Hey, Clarence. What are you guys doing downstairs? You're all so quiet."

My face started to burn. "It's a new game."

"Oh." He put his book down. "I hope it's fun."

I shrugged and looked out the window. It was still coming down sideways and wet. A truck and van drove by with mattresses of snow on top of them. I had a flash of asking Mr. Sparrow to drive me home, but that pizza smelled so good. Maybe I could eat and then go home if things got stupider.

"So your folks are at the hand games and drum dance, hey?" Mr. Sparrow asked.

I felt my stomach sink. "I'm not sure."

He looked at me. "I may head out there later."

I nodded.

"It's amazing how Smith changed ever since we hosted the sundance out at the Fox Holes, hey?" he asked.

I nodded again. I had seen Mr. Sparrow at the community meeting years ago when it was announced the sundance was coming to town. Mr. Sparrow was Native. I wasn't sure which kind, but it felt good to see someone so proud of it.

"Remember that guy who came to the meeting and he was making fun of the pipe carrier?" I asked.

"Yeah," he said. "Spotted Eagle sure told him off, hey?"

A medicine man from the south named Spotted Eagle said he had a dream—a vision, in which a tree told him that this was the place: the people were hurting and Fort Smith was to host a sundance for four years every August to help heal our community.

"Who is this guy who thinks he can bring a ceremony from the south here?" one guy asked at our table.

"This isn't our way," an old trapper said.

"But what is our way?" Mr. Sparrow stood and said. "We have new poisons in our community. Crack, crystal meth, pills. If this promotes healing and getting us to remember who we are with the church and without it, I say we host our guests who are on their way."

And a lot of people cheered.

Spotted Eagle was there in our town. He had had long white hair. He didn't look Aboriginal but he had a nose that was sharp. I bet it could cut butter. He had a choker on and a belt with blue stones. He was carrying a peace pipe that had a feather tied to it.

He was about to speak and address the crowd when a drunk man walked in. "Hey, Chief," he said. "I wanna be a pipe carrier, too. How do you greedy Treaties do it?"

"My friend," the man said. "When you can hold a mountain in one hand and a forest in the other, then you're starting to understand the responsibility—"

"Ah, shut up," he said. "Show me one Indian who isn't Catholic. You should all be grateful for the church, you dirty Indians."

Two of the men who work for the town pushed the drunk man out and that's when my folks said I should go. Brutus was with me and we left to play in our tree fort.

"Yeah, I remember," I said.

"Well, look," Mr. Sparrow said. "Now there's Cree and Chip being taught at the Early Start. Smith is doing great at the hand games. We got drum practice every Wednesday at the Friendship Centre. That sundance woke us up and got us to remember who we are with and without the church." He paused and looked at me. "I guess we're all children of the sundance now."

I nodded. That was a new phrase everyone said: "with or without the church." It was respectful, kind of like the Saturday Night Request Show. Before when Native men used to call in and they'd be drinking, they'd say, "I had a hard life you know…I had a hard life," before they made their request or "requess" as they said. But now, after the sundance came, they all say, "I'm on my healing journey, hey…I'm on my healing journey." Me and my mom would always laugh when they said it. "Boyyyyyy," we'd say together and my dad would shake his head.

I remember the first year, after we went to witness the sundance, we drove out as a family. My parents held hands and walked towards the tree. I got shy about it and asked if I could help out with serving the elders. I could see a tree far off wrapped in blankets of colour. It looked like a huge butterfly in blues and reds, yellows and greens. The whistles. I think it was eagle whistles were going on and on. I wasn't exactly scared. I was just…respectful of it.

That night, after we got home, Mom made Dad a beautiful sheath for his hunting knife out of moosehide and she even did some beadwork on it. I don't know where he keeps it, but you can bet it's his most prized possession.

I looked around the Sparrow home. When I got older, I wanted a home just like this: it looked normal on the outside, but inside it was like a log home. There were books everywhere and the radio was always on. Maybe that was why Blaire read so much. His dad liked Zane Grey and had many bookshelves to hold hundreds of Western books. When I got older, I was going to have a house like that: filled with everything I loved.

"You know," Mr. Sparrow said, "Beth and I give thanks every day you guys take such great care of Blaire. He sure had a rough go until you two came along. This town is not kind if you have a speech impediment."

I nodded. "Blaire's fun."

"He's our pride and joy," he smiled and got up. "Want some milk?"

"Yes, please," I beamed.

I looked on the wall. There were pictures of Blaire from when he was a baby all the way up until now. Every Christmas, it seemed, they'd get a family portrait at the Northern. I studied the ones taken recently and you could see his moles spreading along his jaw. I shook my head. It wasn't his fault.

I heard the freezer door close and the glasses being set up.

"Where's Mrs. Sparrow?" I asked politely. The house seemed quiet.

"Oh," he said. "Prayer group. It's a sad story but one of the town drunks froze to death out by the airport."

I nodded. "Yeah. I heard about that."

"Strange. He must have been on a blackout and thought he was walking home."

I shivered about this because the last time we all tried to astral project, Treyton and Blaire both said the spirit above them grabbed and carried them both to a patch of forest by the airport, before the trailer park and there was a man face up with ice in his mouth. His eyes were gone cuz of the ravens. And two days later we all learned of the body being discovered.

Spooky! I realized my hands were freezing and I could hear talking downstairs through the vents. I leaned closer to listen but it was muffled.

"I like your hat," Mr. Sparrow pointed with his lips towards the closet where I'd hung it up. "Is it muskrat?"

Richard Van Camp

"Yeah," I said. Brutus's mom, Mercy, gave it to me for her last Christmas.

"I had a hat like that once," he walked back into the living room. "The last time I wore it I just about froze to death."

"What?" I took a sip of the milk and it was ice cold and sweet. Perfect!

"Yup," he continued. "I was on a sled when I was a kid. We were outside of Fort Res. I wanted to be a big kid and I kept saying I could hold on for the forty-minute skidoo ride back. Well, they trusted me and that was a mistake. I got bumped off about halfway there and they kept going. Nobody knew I had fallen off. It was a community hunt. Caribou. I wasn't dressed properly and, you know, looking back, when you freeze to death, you get sleepy and warm. It's so peaceful. It's actually the easiest thing to let go and surrender."

I put the drink down. I felt bad we were talking like this. The funeral would be Sunday. Maybe that man's spirit was listening. What was sad was he was blind. Maybe that dark spirit floated above him as he walked alone, leading him to his very last footsteps.

"Wanna know how I beat it?" he asked me.

I could hear yelling in the basement but I wasn't sure if it was Blaire or Treyton. Why were they yelling?

"My great-aunt had just passed and she kept yelling at me from the spirit world to wake up or I'd die. She actually — no word of a lie — pushed me up and helped me walk.

"Wow," I said. "How old were you?"

"The exact age you are now. Hey, can you ask Brutus to call me? We're out of fish and I want to place an order with his dad."

I grimaced and looked out the window. "Sure."

"It must be tough without his mom, hey?"

That was a horrible day when I did what I did. I finally worked up my courage to go out for fries and gravy and coffee with Treyton and Blaire at the Corkscrew restaurant. I knew Brutus would be looking for me and so did Treyton and Blaire. "Look," Treyton said. "Brutus and his family: they're pretty chiefy, hey?"

They lived out in Indian Village. They had a shack for a house and a dog team out back. "So?"

"He and I don't get along. Never did. Blaire and I think it's time you make a choice."

Blaire nodded.

I sat up. "What choice?"

"Well," Treyton said. "You have to choose. If he comes here, prove to us that we're number one in your book."

"We can tell when you hang with him," Blaire said.

"How?" I asked.

"You smell like smoke," Treyton wrinkled his nose.

"Why can't I be friends with everyone?"

Treyton and Blaire shook their heads. "No," Treyton said. "That's not how it works. My sister said Roy Bartleman and his crew are already watching the up-and-comers for the parties for next year. Do you or don't you want to be invited?"

My face burned. Hanging with Treyton and Blaire was fun, most of the time. They had toys, Xbox, games. Brutus wasn't into toys: he was into hunting, trapping, checking nets. When I went over there, we worked: hauled wood, cut kindling, watched him skin animals. They had a woodstove and they were always smoking meat in and outside of the house. That's why we smelled of smoke every time we were in their home. It was great dry meat, boy!

"Prove to us, Clarence, you're one of us," Treyton said. "I'll give you my favourite shirt."

"You can keep the bra-bum pants," Blaire said.

Wow! Treyton's shirt was from West Edmonton Mall. It said Gap on the inside. He let me wear it one day and Sharon, Marcy and Janine all came up and ran their hands up my arms. "Nice shirt," they said. I got dizzy from all the attention. It was Blaire who told me one day I had an Indian bum but that he could loan me a pair

of pants that would push my bum cheeks together like a bra. And it
was true. When I wore them, I had a bum. When I didn't, I'd shuf-
fle around all day with my cheeks clenched so hard I gave myself
the stucks!

Just then, Brutus walked into the restaurant with his gumboots
on and his torn jeans and jean jacket. He had a big pair of binoculars with him. "Hey, guys," he said. He pulled up a seat, turned
it around, sat on it and took a sip out of my coffee cup. Treyton
and Blaire frowned. Brutus also helped himself to our fries and gravy and dragged his sleeve into the mix. "Mmm," he said. "Deadly
fries, hey?"

He took another sip out of my coffee and patted his knees. "Wanna
go in the tree fort?" he asked.

I looked to Treyton and Blaire. They looked down. "Uh," I said.

"Or we could go see the pelicans down at the rocks," he said.
"They might have their babies out."

That sounded great, actually.

"Yeah," Treyton said and kicked me under the table. "We have
plans."

"Oh," Brutus said. "Whatcha think, Clarence?" He took another
sip and dribbled all over his chin. He wiped his face with his sleeve
before going to town on the fries and gravy.

I was suddenly embarrassed to be around him. He looked rough
and he did smell of smoke. Worse today, he smelled of fish slime.

I could feel Blaire and Treyton glaring at me. "I'll be right back,"
I said.

I stood and walked towards the bathroom, but I hooked a right
and walked out the side entrance, careful to not close the door all the
way. I raced around the building and found his bike, the bike Brutus
sold a lynx pelt for. I whipped out my thumb knife and slashed the
back tire. "I'm sorry, buddy," I said and walked away.

I doubled back and made it back into the restaurant pretending to
wipe my wet hands on my pants. "Wanna go see the pelicans?" I asked.

Treyton and Blaire looked at me with horror. "Come on," I said. As Brutus bent over to finish up the fries, I winked at Blaire and Treyton. They looked at each other suspiciously.

"You can pay," Treyton said and I did. My face burned as I realized what was about to happen.

"Let me get my bike," Brutus said.

Treyton sighed and Blaire looked up. "Pelicans," he pointed. We looked and there they were: a squadron of them soaring high above us. It was a beautiful day and I kept looking up, dreading the next few moments that were about to change everything. My eyes started to water with the guilt that was trickling into me and all of my soul.

"No way," Brutus yelled. "Oh man."

I wiped my eyes on my shirt and blinked. "What?"

"My back tire," he pointed. He looked around. "Oh, man. I must have run over some glass."

Treyton and Blaire looked to me and I pointed to my pocket. They looked to each other and grinned.

"Oh man," he said. "How'm I gonna get home?"

"Can you call your dad?" I asked. I wanted to put my hand on his shoulder. I wanted to say I was sorry. I wanted to help him with everything I had, but it was too late.

"Aww," he said, looking to the government building. "My auntie works at Manpower. I'll ask if she can call." He hung his head. "I hope my dad doesn't get mad at me."

Brutus's dad didn't cut him any slack when things like this happened, especially after Mercy passed. "Take care of your things and they'll take care of you," was one of his mottos. He also said things like, "The quickest way to get something broken is to lend it out." I also heard him say, "Wanna lose a friend quick? Lend them money."

Brutus's dad's lungs sounded like wrinkled dragonfly wings now. They crackled when he breathed and his face was grey. Still he smoked; still he drank. Quiet for days at his table looking down. He was one of those Indians who turned more and more purple the more he drank, and his breath got sweeter and sweeter as he did. It was sad. One time after Mercy passed, I walked to Brutus's to see how he was doing, and I could hear drumming coming from the kitchen: two drums. I bet it was Brutus and his dad. I felt so bad for them that I walked home.

"Ah," he said. "You guys go ahead. Here." He took his binoculars out. "Take 'em. Let me know if you see any babies." He offered them to Treyton.

"Thanks," Treyton said and he motioned for Blaire to take them.

"Okay," he said. "Sorry, guys. I gotta go."

"Are you sure?" I asked. "Like, can we help?"

"Clarence," Treyton said. "He said he's fine. Let's go."

"Yeah," Blaire said.

I looked at Brutus who was looking at his tire. He looked so sad. "Sorry, bud," he said. "I wanted to double you home."

That was the moment all the tendons and sinews of my heart snapped. I knew Treyton and Blaire were watching my every move. I could feel it. These were the seconds that counted. "You'll be okay," I said. "See you later?" I wanted to say, but didn't. I knew if I said it I'd have to prove myself all over again, and I could only do this cut once. It had to be public like this. It had to be the slice of forever.

I started walking away with Treyton and Blaire with Brutus's binoculars. I wanted to throw up with what I'd done.

As we walked down Field Street towards the Welfare Center, towards the trails that lead to rapids and pelicans, Treyton started to giggle. "How did you do it?"

I closed my eyes, pressed them shut as hard as I could and produced my thumb knife.

"Whoah," Blaire said. "Ninja!"

"Lemme see," Trey said. "Cool."

This was the knife that was given to me my birthday. My mom gave me rat root for protection. She later sewed it into the hem of my parka. It was a small party but I'd never felt prouder to be Tlicho.

That was when Brutus gave me the muskrat hat that Mercy made for me. She made two before she passed: one for him and one for me. Brutus's dad already had one but I had a dream soon after that I could see him trying the one that was meant for me over and over, crying, trying to make it fit.

"Okay. You're in," Blaire said. "You showed us."

"Yup," Treyton said. "You'll get the shirt tomorrow."

"Keep the pants," Blaire said.

I'd burn the shirt. I knew I'd never wear it. The pants...well, I'd keep the pants.

Trey handed me the knife and the binoculars. "They stink," he wrinkled his nose.

I smelled it and inhaled as much as I could. I didn't know the exact number of muskrats Brutus had to skin to get it, but I could smell the smoke on it, the smoke of dry meat, spruce, hot tea and bannock.

Brutus, I thought. *I'm so sorry. Who will you have now?*

All of a sudden, we heard a bang in the basement, like someone falling off the couch.

"Hey now," Mr. Sparrow stood. "What's going on down there?"

"Our new game," I said. "We shoot catapults at our He-Men."

The timer went off on the stove and he stood. "Tell those boys supper's ready."

"Okay," I said and made a run for it.

I crept quietly to the door.

"Don't you tell him," Treyton said. "It's not his fault."

"Well, he has to know," Blaire said.

"What can he do about it?" Trey asked.

"Nothing," Blaire answered.

What the heck were they talking about? I knocked on the door.

"Hey," Treyton called. "Come in."

I walked in and it was Treyton and Blaire who looked down.

"Supper's ready," I said, hoping this would make them forget about the game.

Blaire held up his hand. "We've decided."

I put my hands in my pockets and felt my cheeks flare with heat. "Okay."

"Clarence," Treyton said, "we've decided this isn't going to work."

"What?"

"You're Indian and that's not gonna change."

I burst out laughing. "Come on."

They both looked at me. "We're serious."

I pointed to the ceiling. "Blaire, your dad's Dene."

He shook his head. "We're Métis."

"So? What does this have to do with anything?"

"Look at your socks," Treyton said.

I looked down. They were wool.

"Only Indians wear those," Trey said.

I looked to him and wanted to see a smirk to show he was kidding. He wasn't.

"Your mom still makes you parkas."

"So what?" I asked.

He shook his head. "Not cool."

"At least I love my mom," I said and I heard a hiss from both of them.

"See?" Treyton looked to Blaire. "What did I tell you? Indians will always backstab you."

Blaire nodded. "You were right."

I felt my voice rise. "Do you have any idea what I did to Brutus to be here? Do you?"

"You backstabbed him," Treyton said. "See? And Blaire and I know your folks are at that big chief drum dance."

"What?" I asked, winded. I started to shake. I knelt down and started grabbing all my He-Mans and my catapult.

"Why did you cover that up?" Blaire asked.

I looked to him through tears. "I told you they were dancing."

He nodded. "But you didn't say they were drum dancing."

I winced. That was true. I didn't want to talk about it.

"Don't be mad," Treyton said. "When you get to high school you can go to the special ed part of the school where they keep the other chiefs."

I looked up at him. I couldn't take him. Blaire would help. The flash of what I'd done to poor Brutus only furthered my sadness. I started to cry.

"I hope that spirit that you keep talking about takes you so high up"—but I stopped. I felt something inside of me, like a trigger—about to be pulled. I marched over to where my parka was and put all my men in the special pockets my mom had made for me on the inside of my parka specifically for each man. I put them in quickly as Blaire walked by to go eat. Beast Man! My Beast Man was upstairs! Ah! Now I'd have to go see Mr. Sparrow and make up some dumb excuse.

Treyton walked by me and paused. "It was a mistake to try and help you." He made his way upstairs and I sat down in a daze as I slowly put all my guys in my pockets and carefully placed Brutus's catapult in the pocket over my heart, and that's when I got mad. To think of what I did to him made me shake. I let out my breath and closed my eyes. Things were about to get ugly—Indian ugly…

I took the pocket knife out of my pocket and cut all of the elastics that held the bodies of Treyton's G.I. Joes together. I also snapped their thumbs off so they'd never hold guns again. For Blaire's He-Men, I cut my knife up and through their leg elastics and crippled them. All of them. I went to slice across their eyes so they'd be blind in this and the spirit world but thought twice. Easy now, I thought. It wasn't their fault.

When I was done, it looked like a death party.

I snapped my knife back in my pocket. I turned and walked upstairs to get my Beast Man. As I took those stairs, I could smell that pizza. It smelled like an outhouse to me now.

Richard Van Camp

"Clarence?" Mr. Sparrow asked. "Are you leaving?"

"Yes, sir," I said. "I have to go."

"There's a bloody blizzard out there," he said.

"It's okay," I said. "I'll walk."

"What happened?" He looked to his son. "I thought this was a sleep over."

Blaire shrugged and kept eating.

"Mr. Sparrow," I said, "thanks for being such great hosts for the pizza parties. You guys were the best. Can I ask you? Are you Slavey or Chip?"

"We're Slavey," he said. "Why?"

"Full blood?" I asked.

"Yes."

I looked at Blaire. He'd paused eating. "Did you know your son hates Indians?"

Mr. Sparrow's head snapped in the direction of Blaire. "What? Is this true?"

Blaire looked down. His face turned bright red. "Treyton does, too."

Mr. Sparrow looked at Treyton and glared. "What the hell happened downstairs?"

I grabbed my Beast Man and put him in my pocket. "I'm sorry, Treyton," I said. "Looks like you're outnumbered. There's Indians everywhere."

"Dirty Indian!" Treyton said.

"Hey!" Mr. Sparrow said.

I didn't stick around to see what happened next. I took the stairs and put on my dad's kamiks and the gloves my mom made me, along with Mercy's muskrat hat. I walked out into the blowing wind and never felt better. It was off to the drum dance for me. Brutus would be there and I'd give him the biggest hug, my mom the biggest kiss and my dad and I would have tea later after Mom went to bed. This storm was nothing.

Tony Toenails

DO YOU EVER WONDER HOW PEOPLE EARN THEIR NICKNAMES? Where I'm from—Fort Smith, NWT—we're the nickname capital of Canada. We have hundreds of nicknames. Some people are born with nicknames; others earn them.

Here's a story my uncle told me one day that I hope makes you laugh. I guarantee you'll be sharing this at the supper table right after you hear it.

There's a couple in town—I can't tell you who they are because I swore to keep it secret, and, ah, you'll know who they are anyway. Okay, what happened, the way I heard it, was like this:

There's this husband and he's the most wonderful husband in the whole wide world. He absolutely adores his wife. He cooks for her, cleans for her, bakes little bannocks. After her yoga class, he runs a bath for her, throws in some Epsom salts and some baby oil. He rubs her little toesie wosies at night with almond butter. He's crazy for her, he sings to her, he writes her a poem every single day. Everything's great! He spoils her. Do you know what I mean? He's so in love, he gives himself a perm just thinking about her!

Anyhow, the only thing is, he has the worst habit ever. It's actually the worst habit in the entire world. (Worse than snoring or leaving the seat up or, um, "arriving early.") He likes his hockey, eh. So when he's watching hockey, every three months, he whips off his socks and he goes, "Aww! Aww! What's going on with my toenails?" He runs his fingers along his scraggly, long, sharp man-hooves. "Ah ha! It's time for me to clip my scragglies!" (That's what he calls them.)

He's a real cheapskate, eh! He doesn't have a big toenail clipper or his own personal one, so he uses his wife's fingernail clipper—the little gold one. So he grinds away, digs away, he cuts and digs and pulls to get under his huge bionic toenails. You know he works out in the bush, eh! So he has his big sweaty toes in wool socks all the time. Imagine these thick yellow toenails with a hint of green. So he clips like this and he clips like that. And they fly, boy! Half of his toenails end up in the goldfish bowl and the other half end up on the plants. As he watches the game, he stops halfway to smell the clipper. That's the man musk right there! That's the aroma of a real man. Oooh hoo! That's the sweet stuff. After he takes another sweet whiff, he goes back to watching the game. His worst habit is, after he clips all his nails, he scoops them up and leaves them on the supper table.

When his wife comes home from work, she is beat. She works hard, eh. She works for the government. She comes home one day and steps on something sharp. It tears right through her sock.

"Ooooh my goodness!" she says. "What is that?"

She pulls from her sock a yellow toenail, all sharp and pokey. She looks at the supper table and there's the biggest pile of yellow toenails piled up curled and jagged. Every three months! And each time this happens, they always have the same fight:

"You have the worst habit in the whole wide world," his wife says. "It's disgusting. I told you to burn your big corn-chip toenails in the wood stove. I shouldn't be stepping on them and cutting up my favourite sock. I may have to get a tetanus shot because of you! I cannot even believe this! If you do that one more time I am going to fix you!"

He says, "Oh baby, baby, I am sorry baby, baby, baby. Don't leave me baby, baby, baby. You're the love of my life. You're my lighthouse, baby, baby, baby. I'll never do it again. I swear!"

And she forgives him and they go into the honeymoon stage, hey. But it happens, she comes home one day three months later. She is having a real rough day, eh, a real rough day. It's election time, hey. She comes home and steps on something sharp again and it rips through her brand new pantyhose. She already knows what it is and she pulls it out. Oh, it is the biggest, grossest toenail. She looks in the fish bowl and the fish are all nibbling on the toenails that plopped in there and half the fish are dead, hey, just floating sideways. She looks at her plants and sees toenails poking through the leaves. She looks at the supper table and there is, once again, that big pile of stinky yellow toenails!

Finally, she snaps. She says, "That's it!"

She scoops up the big pile of toenails and doesn't say a word. Oh, it stinks, eh! She hides this big yellow pile of scraggly toenails in the Lazy Susan, right at the back. The next morning she makes his lunch. She decides to teach him a lesson. She has bread and butter, mayonnaise, baloney—because he is quality, eh! Quality knows quality. Five stars all the way. Then, as he sings a love song for her from the shower, she takes his toenails and sprinkles them all over the baloney. Then she takes some cheese, then some lettuce, now some mustard and some butter and another piece of bread. She pushes it down and the toenails poke right through the bread like thick barbed thorns. She wraps the toenail sandwich in Saran Wrap and then she gets a little juice box, a little chocolate pudding, a thermos of tea, and she puts it in his lunch box. She gives him a little kiss and says, "Baby, baby, baby, have a good day baby, baby. I love you, I love you. You're the love of my life. Bye."

And her man goes to work. About five minutes later, she goes, "Oh my God! What if he chokes on his own toenails! Oh my God!" She calls his boss. She says, "Whatever happens—as soon as my husband comes in—just get him to call home. It's an emergency."

The boss says, "Oh, ah, oh—I won't forget." Well guess what? He forgot.

Her husband worked out in the bush. Just like I told you. He's a heavy-machine operator in great big sweaty clothes all day, and lovely wool socks to get his toes just nice and stinky, hey. His wife is sweating bullets all day, worried her hubby will choke on his own toenails. She's in agony with worry!

Richard Van Camp

Well, he comes home at six o'clock. His wife is running around the house. Oh thank God! He's alive; he's safe.

"Baby, baby, baby!" She said, "You're the love of my life! You're my lighthouse! I have tea; I have coffee; I made buffalo chili here with bannock. I even have Kraft Dinner because it's your favourite. I made apple pie for you because I love you so much baby, baby, baby. How was work?"

"WOW!" her hubby said. "All right! I could get used to this. This is great! Wait—is it your birthday?"

"No!" his wife said.

"Our anniversary?" he asked.

"Nope," his wife beamed.

"What's the big occasion?" he asked.

"Our love," she said. "Our love is the big occasion! What other reason do I need to spoil my man?"

"Oh hey!" her husband said. "That sounds good. That sounds really good."

"How was your lunch?" his wife asked.

"Lunch?" he asked. "What lunch?"

"The lunch that I made you," she said.

And he went, "Oh, I don't know. I had a tummy ache. I gave it to Tony."

His best friend ate his toenails! Hoo hoo! Can you imagine? Can you imagine his best friend Tony munching on his sandwich going: "Wow this is so crunchy. Wow! Oh that crunch. Oh yeah. So good. Oh wow. Are those chips or fish bones or what? Oh so good. So good! Mmmmm."

And now you know how Tony Toenails got his nickname. We're so very proud to add another nickname to the growing pile around here.

Love Song

RAY PEARCE AND I WERE AT TOWN HALL WATCHING THE PROCEEDINGS —mainly we go for the free coffee and bannock, but we also go for the free entertainment as the mayor and the ex-mayor go toe-to-toe on some of the problems facing our community in the land of "Wah-s," "Take it easy-s," "Cheap-s," and "Fuck sakes anyways-s." For example, the bison issue in Wood Buffalo National Park is a very prickly area when it comes to politics. Charles Chaplin, the mayor of Fort Smith, wanted to leave the bison alone. That's just fine except that the bison have bovine brucellosis and tuberculosis. They're bleeding from themselves and they got pus in their knee joints. If we see one staggering out on the highway, we—wah! I mean the hunters—usually shoot so as to put it out of its misery, and if you're a hunter handling the meat and you got a cut on your finger you can get what they got. Anyway, Oops!, the ex-mayor of Fort Smith and now chief, started to hoop and holler about what was going to be done about the bison.

Mayor Chaplin, I guess, is ready for any such opposition. He starts off real slow and stands up to greet the crowd. He says, "Ladies and gentlemen, as mayor of Fort Smi—"

"BULLSHIT!" somebody snaps from the crowd. We all look and it's Oops! who leans heavy on one knee and glares at Mayor Chaplin.

Mayor Chaplin takes a long, slow swig on his coffee and swishes it through his teeth. He's got a trumpet mouth happening; nobody says a thing. He stands up and glares at Oops!. Mayor Chaplin starts up again with a cheesy smile on his face, one that says he can take a little heckling. "Please," he says, sticking his hands up, showing he's a friend of the people. "Please understand that this issue is not black and whi—"

"BULLSHIT!" Another cry from the audience and, sure enough, it's Oops!. This time he glares right back at Mayor Chaplin whose lips are twitching with that crazy vein of his under his left eye throbbing. He swallows hard and pulls that cheesy grin tight. It looks like he's either in sweet agony or he's in the throes of a lengthy bowel movement. Everybody in the room knows he wants to give Oops! a lickin', but it's election year and the press is in the room. He tightens his belt and tucks in his shirt. He says, "Order! Order. I'm trying to explain the direction of movement on the issue."

He tries to say more but Oops! stands and yells, "YOU WOULDN'T MOVE IF SOMEONE STUCK A FIRECRACKER UP YOUR ASS!"

"THAT'S IT, YOU SUMABITCH!" Mayor Chaplin roars and charges. Everybody stands and holds him off. Oops!, seeing that it is now safe to do so, charges too and everybody in the middle gets squished. Ladies run around all panicky. Me and Ray crack jokes and wait for someone to call order. It can get pretty hairy sometimes, but it's cheaper than bingo and the mayor's wife makes damn good bannock.

Fuck sakes anyways: I know exactly how this re-election's going to go. The Chaplins are the biggest family in town and Oops! knows it. So he gets great business out at his hardware store by sniping from the sidelines. In fact, it's safe to say he's built his business by going after Mayor Chaplin for years. Cheap.

So Ray Pearce and I, we're sitting together waiting for everyone to cool down when Conrad Blitz walks in with one of the prettiest women I have ever seen. This woman that Conrad has is Asian, and she is something bee-u-tee-ful. We're talkin' walkin' porcelain. Her face is so pretty, her hair a running black. She's so tiny. Her head is bowed, looking only at her feet. She keeps herself close to Conrad who sticks his ape face out at anyone who's checking her out. He looks like a mean old gorilla walking around. He has three big rings that look like gold nuggets. He has his shirt buttons undone so we can practically see his belly button, and he wears that big key chain that makes lots of noise whenever he walks into the room.

"Jeezus," Ray says to me. "Will you look at her? My oh my, Grant, I ain't never seen someone so lovely. Look at her."

Every man at the meeting who's been rolling cigarettes or sipping coffee eyeballs her really soft-like. Conrad sits down with her and she sits quick, kinda like she's shy to be there.

Conrad works at Stud Concrete. I don't know what it is he does over there. I only know that he caught my cousin siphoning gas from one of his haul-trucks and Conrad put him in the hospital. I heard he also got one of his men to hold Ronny's head up while he brought those rings down and down into his face. Shattered his jaw. Cut the inside of his gums up. Deviated his nose. Charges were never pressed despite me begging. The family swore to keep it quiet. That was a year ago and I've been biding my time to get him back. I just can't figure on how he got this lady cuz she sure is something.

Blitz grunted something to the lady and she shot up real quick and got him a coffee. All the while she only looks up once to see where the coffee maker is. Other than that, she keeps that pretty head of hers down. Damn she's tiny. Jet black hair pulled tight in a ponytail, pouting lips and huge eyes, something that you'd see on a doe: scared, alert. Blitz grins wide and shows us he's the boss.

"Jeezus, will you look at that. Conrad Blitz got himself a slave," I say to Ray.

I get no answer from Ray so I look over. Ray's got an expression on his face like he's a school kid who's fallen in love. His big puppy eyes have little hearts in them and he sighs loud and slow. Blitz sees Ray looking and leans towards him, giving him the buffalo-eye, but Pearce keeps on starin'. About that time the lady, who looks like a China doll, brings Blitz his coffee. She keeps standing, looking down with that cup in her small hands. Blitz goes to turn and shoulders the cup. A lot of that coffee runs down his shirt and he shoots straight up slapping it like it's liquid fire. His little China doll tries to help but Blitz slams his fist into her.

"Get me something to wipe it with!" Everyone stops talking when he raises his voice to her. Mrs. Chaplin helps her with the paper towels. Others move the chairs aside and Blitz doesn't like all of the attention so he ups and stomps out of the room without saying anything to the lady. She's on her knees wiping it up like real quick. She uses one towel and then another. She's getting soaked cuz she's on it but all the while she cleans. Ray Pearce up and bolts over; he kneels down beside her and says something. China doll keeps working and Ray helps her out. Then he takes her tiny hand and helps her up. He says something soft and she smiles. Even with her head bowed, that smile lights up the room. Everybody's happy after that and people come up and introduce themselves hoping to find out more about her.

"*Tansi!* Hello. How are you? Where you from? What do you think of our little town?"

She shakes all their hands and bows. She smiles and talks quietly. Ray Pearce stands beside her and he's beaming a smile from ear to ear. He's all proud and introduces her to everyone. Turns out her name is Swee-Sim Blitz. We all get a handshake and a look when Blitz comes back. We hear his steel-toed boots and the ching ching ching of that big key chain. He pushes through everyone, grabs China doll and takes her outside. She has her head back down and her ponytail goes up and down, up and down as she gallops behind him.

Everyone goes back to quiet in their seats. Oops! and the mayor settle down and call the meeting to a close, but Ray Pearce is shaking, his lower lip trembling. The look in his eyes makes me remember something I almost forgot. When I was a kid, I used to play this game called "Let me be you for a night." In it, I'd always fantasize about being a woman's husband for one night. The things I'd do... well, let's just say if I had that *inkwo* I bet I could save a lot of marriages. The look in Ray's eyes, though. I think it was safe to say he wanted to play that game and break whatever Blitz had brewing with Fort Smith's new secret. And me? I'd help him every step of the way. This was my ticket to retribution for Ronny.

We all go out to the driveway. There's a fresh bed of snow out in the parking lot, but we're all too quiet to care. The snow looks blue at night and I'm bundled up pretty good. The way it's falling, it looks like thousands of moths dying, falling to earth — sky feathers, I'm sure our ancestors called them. I walk home and Ray roars by in his truck. He peels out of that driveway and heads way out of town to where he stays.

Within a day, I hear through the moccasin telegraph that Blitz got himself one of them mail-order brides. I guess you get a catalogue and you just fill out an order form. The funny thing is, she's been in town about eight months. Usually, it's advertised in the paper when someone new comes to town, but I guess this is hush-hush as Blitz lives in Border Town, a small mysterious settlement across the highway towards the park. We streaked by there a few times this past fall and it always struck me as a good place for a bear attack or an ambush of muskets and arrows. That dirty fucker. Can you imagine that first night he got her in his house? The things he made her do? Imagine his big fuckin' beer belly bouncing off her forehead every night. Fuck him. I fuckin' hate Conrad so much. This gives me more fuel for my plans.

Friday night rolls around and we have our annual talent show contest. Brutus and Clarence don't show so they must be tokin'. Ever since Clarence became a dad, well, I don't really see him anymore and when he does go out, it's with Brutus to Panty Point for a hoot. *Why do they never call me?* And Brutus and Sheri are shacked up now. They're probably just barebacking it around in their home right now. Man, I miss streaking with my dog brothers through the night. I am so fucking bored at night now that I actually floss.

The talent contest is always held in the church basement. The parking lot is full of trucks and skidoos. Every year, it's the same: Buckets and his wife jig to fiddle music. Buckets's wife beat cancer so we all stand and cheer her on. Plus, the Red River Jig is a crowd pleaser every time. Their little feet shoot out from under them real quick and everyone claps and cheers them on. Some of the teenagers put together a band called Savage Society. They pull out electric guitars and start jamming real loud. That's when the judges and elders go for a smoke break.

Next up is a girl group called GLOSS. The girls all look thirteen and are all wearing what looks like their mothers' makeup and high heels. "Want to know what GLOSS stands for?" the lead singer asks the crowd. "Guys Love Our Sassy Stuff!"

The crowd laughs and they cover a Britney Spears song but half the band forgets the lyrics and runs off the stage and then the lead singer realizes what's happened so she runs off the stage too, and well, that was interesting.

Then some other people get up on stage. They come from Fort Chip and Fort Fitz. This one guy comes up on stage and plays a saw like a violin. It sounds all weepy and sad. He plays "Amazing Grace" and we all stand. Don't ask me why we stand; it just sounds so good.

I look around for any potentials, but no dice. A few new faces but not my type. Cheap.

After that, Mayor Chaplin crawls up on stage and asks us how we're doing. He starts talking about how nice it is to see everyone lending support to the local talent and our visitors from other communities. Then he starts talking about all the things he's going to do if he gets re-elected, like pave the highway clear to Enterprise, like set up another baseball diamond (we already have five but everyone cheers anyway) and on and on.

He would've kept on going if Oops! hadn't yelled, "Keep it short!" Everyone claps because what he hollered is what we all were thinking. He stands up and takes a bow. Mayor Chaplin cuts it short and introduces the next act. "Okay, okay," he says, waving his hands. "Coming to you tonight, for your evening pleasure, for the first time ever, our very own Fort Smith historian—the man who knows it all: Ray Pearce!"

Everybody claps and I spit out my coffee. Ray? Jeezus, I've known Ray for about five years and I know how he hates crowds. The spotlight shines on the stage and there he is. He stumbles to the podium and Mayor Chaplin adjusts the mike. Ray looks pretty fancy up there in a moosehide jacket. He must be pretty hot but I don't see any sweat. He composes himself and takes a deep breath. Everybody takes one with him and we see this is mighty important. We're all quiet and everybody hushes one another.

"My first story tonight is about how the Dogrib people came to be," he says, making eye contact left and right like a lighthouse, making sure everyone understands what's going on. I take a big breath. The Dogrib are outnumbered here in Smith: a town that's Dene, Cree, French and English. If anyone heckles him, I might have to go bazook—

"A long time ago, when medicine power was the law and the way of the Dene people, a woman gave birth to six dog-pups. This woman was very beautiful. Nobody knew who the father was so she lived all alone in the bush. She was very happy to be living by herself because she loved her children very much.

"Every day, before she would go out to check her rabbit snares, she would put her pups in a bag and tie it up so they wouldn't get into trouble while she was gone, and every day she would come home with her catch and she would see baby-human footprints in the snow outside her camp. She would rush inside her tent and check to see if all her pups were okay. They were still tied up in their little bag and they would all start to yap so she would feed them."

Ray pauses and takes a sip of water that someone brought to him while he was talking. "So one day, she decided to see who it was making the baby tracks outside her lodge. A little while passed and, sure enough, she could hear children laughing and playing. But it was not from outside the tent. It was from inside. And then, from the moosehide teepee, six young children came running out. They played naked outside in the snow and they were just as happy as could be. The mother watched this and sprang from the bush. She chased them back into the tent and caught the last ones before they could leap into the bag. The other babies turned back into dogs but the ones she captured stayed human. And those were the first Dogrib Indians. As you know, they call themselves Tlicho."

People look at each other with wide eyes and clap like thunder. I puff my little bony chest out and nod. Yup, that was our creation story, our beginning story. The way my mom told it though: the woman grabbed two boys and a girl and they never changed back, but I hear there's three versions of our story. Ray takes another sip from his water and he begins again. "The second story I want to tell you was told to me by the chief of Hay River. It's about a spring ceremony and women."

Everybody gets quiet again and listens. I notice the kids are all sitting down. Some are with their parents. A bunch sit down at the front.

"A long time ago," he says, "women of Denendeh used to have a spring ceremony. They would go off by themselves for four days every year. When they came back to the village, the ceremony was never spoken of. Men had no knowledge of what took place and were not permitted to ask. During the ceremony, men could hear singing and chanting. They could hear animals sometimes singing along with the women."

People look at each other with astonishment. There's lots of nods all around me and everyone's listening now.

"I guess there was one year when one of the younger men called the other men together. 'What's going on over there?' he asked. 'Every year this happens and yet we know nothing of what takes place. For four days, we watch the kids and we cook and we clean. That's women's work. How come they get to take this time for themselves when we should be hunting?' The younger men agreed, but the elders tried to tell him that he should respect the women's privacy. The young man ignored his elders. He left early the next morning to spy.

"That night, as the men listened, there was a horrible noise. It was a man screaming, screaming in pain. His screaming was heard for miles. It was followed by an incredible silence that echoed for days.

"Soon after, the women walked back to the settlement. They were covered in blood. They all walked down to the water and washed before returning to their families. They carried on like nothing bad had happened. The men were too scared to ask about this. A few of the hunters wondered where the young man was. Finally, the men left to go look for him.

"They went to the place where the women held their ceremony and they found a field picked clean of any grass, any weed, any berry. Even the birds and mice wouldn't cross it. It was just dirt: black, black dirt.

"They never found the man who went to spy on the women. They never found his body or heard from him ever again.

"That field I'm telling you about is in Fort Providence. Birds won't even fly over it. The animals walk around it, and that haunted earth remains barren even to this day."

Everybody gasps and "aaahhh." Then we all stand and cheer. I sip my coffee and she's gone cold. "When men intrude on woman power, the Dene and the land suffer," I think he says through the applause.

I sit back down and get ready for more. This time the elders move up to the front and everybody comes in from the cold outside. Ray takes another sip and starts again. "I'm going to ask for your help in my last story."

Uh-oh. Everybody gets nervous and giggly. I look down at my boots and pray he doesn't ask for volunteers or get us to lock arms and sway as we sing something.

"I need a volunteer," he says.

Everybody blushes and looks around. "Who's it gonna be?" Ray hops off the stage and goes into the crowd. I see him stand off to the front left of the crowd and offer his hand to someone in a parka. His hand is met and someone stands up. He takes her up on stage. At first, I think he grabbed one of the Wandering Spirit girls, but then I see it's her: Swee-Sim. *Uh oh*, I think. *Where's Conrad?* She has a wolverine-trimmed parka with a purple shell and mukluks that are so small.

She wears her hair down and it flows like black water over the hood. She is smiling and looking down. Many people lean left and right to get a better look and they all ask who she is.

Ray grabs the mike and says, "Ladies and gentlemen, I'd like you to give a warm welcome to Swee-Sim Blitz." Everybody cheers and stomps their feet. He asks her something and she answers. "Swee-Sim's from China and her husband's not here." Everybody watches her and she looks down, blushing. "Okay now," Ray says, "I'm glad your hubby isn't here because now I can hold your hand." Everybody laughs and Ray smiles. He has a twinkle in his eye and he's blushing but he powers through and says, "In the olden days, there were arranged marriages."

Everybody in the crowd nods and remembers.

"If you could hunt and provide for yourself and a family, you were considered a prime person, ripe for marriage."

The lights dim and Ray continues. "Sometimes, though, people didn't get the person they fell in love with. Maybe the parents didn't think too highly of one boy and thought highly of another. Well, that girl, she's heartbroken, but she goes with it because that was how it was done in the olden days. But somewhere along the way, the people invented the Love Song. And now I'm going to sing this for all of you." He says it to everyone, but he's looking at Swee-Sim.

I look around. Conrad is nowhere to be seen.

Ray puts down his mike and lets go of Swee-Sim's hand. He grabs a drum from behind the stage and holds up the stick in his other hand. Some people bow their heads and others make the sign of the cross. Ray hits that drum slow and he starts to sing to her. Swee-Sim keeps looking down and he starts off so soft. He goes like this:

Hah gee lah nee haaay
Hah gee lah nee haaay
Hah gee lah nee haaay
Hah gee lah nee haaay

He hits that drum like a heartbeat and he keeps it going. He says it over and over and looks at all of us. Soon we're all singing along and everyone holds hands. I get real warm inside and we raise our voices to meet the night. I watch Swee-Sim and she's singing, too. She looks up straight at him, not afraid, and her little frame starts to sway.

Hah gee lah nee haaay
Hah gee lah nee haaay

I feel real strong inside, like something's so right. I get all choked and keep on singing. Ray keeps it going and, after a while, he walks Swee-Sim back to her seat. He turns and walks back to the stage. When he gets back up, he bows and keeps going. When he gets quiet and we think he's gonna stop, he takes a deep breath and goes real loud, like a tide. Soon he stops. Everyone keeps singing without a drum and it sure sounds pretty.

After that, it gets quiet and everyone makes the sign of the cross again. One of the elders next to me turns off to the side and wipes his face. He steadies himself up on a cane and walks out. People stand and cheer and we all come back to earth. Everybody shakes hands. Old friends say hi and even Mayor Chaplin and Oops! shake hands with each other, and I get a few hugs, just for being me. Soon, the mayor comes out and tells everyone the winners. Ray won hands down and everyone claps and hollers. Everyone leaves after that so they can get out of stacking chairs and cleaning.

I go to find Ray but the mayor says he left real quick. I go out to the parking lot and there he is. He's getting handshakes all around and in the truck — shotgun — is Swee-Sim. It looks to me like she's smiling really quiet and I know that everything's okay in the world, but, as I walk home under the twirling and tickly snow, I wonder how this will all play out: how will he get her away from Blitz? I drop tobacco outside my trailer and ask for the angels to take her away and put her in the arms of a man who could give her the world — the right way.

Ray's performance was in the paper and even on the CBC. I guess someone taped it and it was played on the radio. It was in the *Slave River Bulletin* but in the picture you can't see Swee-Sim. All you see is Ray talking serious in one picture and him holding the drum in the other. I wondered what she told Conrad about her night out.

Work picked up at the jail. I'm a guard and our own people are bringing in the hillbilly heroin of oxycontin, crack cocaine, and crystal meth. It's my job now to protect the prisoners from each other and themselves. It was after four nights of C Shifts when I heard from Ray again. It was on the phone.

"Grant!" he says like a little kid. "We gotta go to the dance this Friday. Blitz is gonna be the DJ. Swee-Sim's gonna be there!"

"Yeah? He gonna let you dance with his wife, or what?"

"Well... I don't know. I kinda asked her to save me a waltz."

"Scoop?"

"I gave her a ride to my house after my stories and I made her tea. We talked about the old ways, things like The Love Song. She sure liked that. So we're going, or what?"

"You bet!" I say. *This is gonna be good.* I slap my hands together. *Prayers are being answered!*

Next Friday, I get a knock on the door. It's Ray all gussied up. He got his hair cut and he's wearing a red checkered shirt. He tells me that's what they used to wear in the old days. It means: "I'm ready, willin' and able." He's got a purple hanky tied around his neck and he sure smells pretty. He's got a wiggle in his step and he's raring to go.

"C'mon! C'mon!" he says like a little kid on Christmas Day. We motor on down in Pearce's old truck. He cleaned it up on the inside and gave 'er a wash on the outside. That's kinda hard cuz it's about thirty below out, but he did it.

We pull up to the Roaring Rapids Hall. She's packed tonight. Usually, people walk to the dance so they can drink and not drive. But it's cold in November and the snow's mighty deep. We make our way.

The music pumps and, sure enough, Blitz is up on stage doing his job. He DJ's sometimes for a little money on the side. He's got a great system. We look for Swee-Sim but she's nowhere to be seen. Ray starts pacing and sweating. I know everyone there so I make my rounds. I get pretty caught up with visiting and dancing. Man, this town can two-step to anything. About two hours pass, and I go outside to cool off. Still no sign of Brutus and Clarence, but then I see her: Swee-Sim.

She was coming from the parking lot carrying a crate of CDs. I run down the stairs and give her a hand. She sure looks pretty in her parka. Underneath, she's all dressed up in a silk dress. Her hair is loose and shiny. She's got a little hush of pink on her cheeks and red lipstick so smooth it makes her lips look delicious. I was about to start up the stairs when Ray put his hand on my shoulder and asks if we need any help. I get the message and say sure. Ole Ray sure takes one heckuva load and leaps up those stairs. He pushes past everyone with Swee-Sim at one arm and that crate in the other. I get back to looking for someone I don't know to flirt with.

When I go back inside, the lights are way down so I kick up my heels and rock with some pretty nice ladies, girls I grew up with. Some are divorced, some are married. We're practically family and there's a peace to seeing everyone growing up together. Soon Blitz plays the last waltz. Somebody in the crowd yells, "Sister Christian!" Everybody hoops and hollers and grabs their partners. I grab Rita, the new x-ray tech who's been giving me the eye all night, and I hug her real close. I sink into Rita's hair and smell her heat and perfume. It's been so long since I worked on my night moves. Gorgeous hips. Strong. I'd love to explore just a little more if it all pans out. I'm about to start my sweet-talkin' when, across the room, I see Ray and Swee-Sim. He has her laughing pretty good and she throws her head back. Ray has that same smile on his face, one that says he wouldn't be anywhere else in the world than right here, right now. He holds her so soft and sure steps lightly. She's kinda short for him but somehow they manage. He twirls her and dips, twirls her and dips. That little hanky he has tied around his neck looks pretty flashy. He sure knows his stuff when it comes to courtin'. I glance at Blitz but he's too busy DJ'ing to notice anything. I get caught up with Rita and start some wandering stuff.

About then, someone slams into me, knocking me down. Someone screams and everything gets fuzzy. All I can see are jeans and shit-kickers. I try to stand but there's too many people. It's dark and I pull my hand close. My ears are ringing and then I hear more people screaming. I pull myself up by a table leg and steady myself. There's Ray and Blitz going at it. Blitz cracks Ray while his mouth is open and Ray drops to the floor. Blitz kicks him while he's down and Swee-Sim's crying for him to stop. I think Blitz would've killed him if the bouncers Boom and Country hadn't jumped him. They haul a roaring Blitz out of there and haul Ray up. Everyone goes outside cuz the dance is over and someone says I'm bleeding. I go to Ray and sees if he's okay. His jaw is out of place and I drive him to the hospital.

Doctor Hoffman sees us in the examining room. Ray's in a lot of pain so the doctor gives him a needle. Ray gets sleepy; his eyes close. I wait three hours and talk with the nurses. They patch me up and give me a coffee. They tell me the doctor's got to wire Ray's jaw shut. I make a joke about how Smith will have some quiet and peace, seeing as Ray does all the yapping. But it isn't funny and nobody laughs.

After a week of A and B shifts, I walk out all the way to Axe Handle Hill to see Ray at his house. It's the same day he was discharged from the hospital. The doctor did a good job and Ray drinks from a straw.

"How you feeling there, little buddy?" I ask.

"Shitty," he says but it comes out like this: "Shshitty."

"I keep waiting for you to come in and press charges on Blitz," I say.

Ray has an intravenous in his arm. He looks and moves likes he's still in a lot of pain and the swelling's down in his jaw, but it's his ribs that hurt. Two broke where Blitz kicked him. Ray doesn't feel like talking so I read him a story. It's a story I've been working on about how Clarence and Brutus and I like to streak in Fort Smith in the summer. Then Ray touches me. He gets his finger to his lips and motions for me to stop. He sits up and we listen.

From outside in the snow we hear a voice. It's soft and I can't make out the words. The voice rises and stops, rises and rests. It sounds like a little kid singing to us. *Dogs? Dog teams?* I look out the window but I can't see anything. Ray motions for me to go outside and check it out. I put on my boots and stomp outside. Without my jacket on, I get cold real quick. I hug myself for warmth and call if anyone's out there. Ray's truck is the only thing I can see. The sky is overcast and I can see the dim face of the moon. The snow is starting to fall and that wind is so fierce it feels like my skin is gonna split. Anyone outside way out here is either gonna freeze or say hello. Still nothing, so I go back inside. Ray tries to stand. "Who the hell's out there?" he asks. "I can still hear it."

"No one. Sit down." And then the phone rings. It's Blitz. He sounds worried; he wants to know where his wife is. This is Day Two of her missing. I tell him I don't know and that he can damn well be sure that Ray's gonna charge his ass as soon as he's better. "We'll see you in JP Court!" I yell. He doesn't say anything for a while and asks to speak to Ray. I tell Ray that Blitz wants to speak to him but Ray just lies down and closes his eyes. Blitz hangs up when I tell him Ray is sleeping.

The next phone call we get is about twenty minutes later. It's the sergeant. He wants to know where Mrs. Blitz is. I tell him what happened and say that Ray is gonna charge Blitz for busting his jaw. Sarge says he'll be right over. I say we'll wait.

When Sarge comes over he's all frog-eyed and scared. He doesn't even knock. He just barges in. I ask him what happened and he says I better get my jacket on. "Something happened. Something awful."

I pull on my boots and parka. Me and Sarge tromp outside and he leads me to his car. I think he's gonna question me, get my statement about the fight, but he stops outside of Ray's truck and shines his flash-light in the cab. "Do you know who this is?"

At first I can't see what's in there but then he opens the door. It's Swee-Sim all busted up. Her eyes are all raccooned and her nose is hammered flat. Three holes have punctured her forehead and I rec-ognize the signature of gold nugget rings. It looks like somebody dug their thumbnails in her skin and scooped the meat out. Those lips of hers are swollen and torn. Her mouth is open in silent awe and I think the top row of her teeth is missing. She's all pale and I can't see any breath from her. She's got claw marks so purple I think she got mauled by a wolverine. I start to shake and tell Sarge we gotta bring her in the house. I pull off my parka and the Sarge tells me it's too late; she's been dead for days.

I hear screaming and I jump. It's Ray and he's standing there in his T-shirt and track pants. The Sarge goes towards him and I hear them. We've woken the sleigh dogs that are tied to their houses across the highway. They're wailing like women and howl for Ray and Swee-Sim.

Everything slows down. *She has been dead for days*. She's frozen solid. *So how did we hear her singing?*

In her small hands is Ray's purple hanky, the one he wore around his neck. She also has a tiny piece of paper and time slows. They have my fingerprints at the cop shop. The Sarge knows who I am. I shield what I'm about to do because I know I was a part of this. Somehow I helped cause this. And I know exactly how this ends. Whatever she wrote will be passed around in the coffee room at the cop shop. It will be read and mocked.

As Sarge holds Ray back from seeing the body and asks me for help, the dogs start screaming but for all the wailing and noise they're making, it doesn't seem loud enough. I take the piece of paper and slip it up my sleeve so Sarge doesn't see. After, when all of this quiets, I will give her last words to Ray on bended knees. And that snow, that snow that looks like thousands of moths dying, the sky feathers bury-ing us all—it just keeps coming down, down, down....

Devotion

I KNOW I'VE.... I KNOW I'VE NEVER BEEN ONE TO BORROW FROM grace before, but the day Charlie went missing, a raven came to me outside my window and tried telling me something. It clucked its beak and started to chatter, and I waved it away, prayed it away. I spoke English; I spoke Dogrib. I even spoke Cree: "*Awas! Awas!*"

Then it gripped its claws on the branch and swung upside down. Looking at me. Clucking. It would not stop trying to tell me something. And that's when I knew: It was Charlie. His spirit, asking for help.

When I was with Charlie we laughed all the time. When I went with him… it was the best time of my life. The way we were. How people loved him. He brightened every room he walked into. People still ask me about him, even after all these years.

When that raven came to me, I had a feeling. Just like when Dad died. I had a feeling. They say many things about the spirit world and here's what I want to say to you. I am going to write this down so you know I know about you, and I'm going to tell you how I figured you out. All of you.

Charlie told me a story one night. It was late. We'd gone dancing. He got into his whiskey. *Just a touch.* That's what he'd say: *just a touch.* And he told me a story. Well, it was a secret. I had been after him for weeks to tell me a secret he'd never told anyone before, and I remember when he started to tell it to me it was because he knew we would be together forever, and that this was the biggest secret of his life.

It went like this. Charlie said a long time ago he was up in the eastern Arctic. "The Artic," he used to call it, and you know how his mother is Eskimo, right? Inuit? He could speak Inuktitut. He could also speak Dogrib. He loved languages. I always meant to ask him what language he dreamt in, but maybe you can for me. You know, Charlie was never the same person after he told me this story.

This happened before he knew me. Charlie said that he was ski-dooing, going to a hunter's camp. It was a beautiful day on Baffin Island. He was making his way and he noticed a camp to his left. The tents were canvas with hides. He passed by and was so excited to go hunting. He had been home for a while with his mom and he was ach-ing for muktuk with soya sauce. Oh he loved to smack his lips when he talked about muktuk and soya sauce. I tried it once with him, and I swear my hair was shiny for a month. It's ever greasy. Oh our kisses were gross after. He loved it. But me, I'll pass....

Anyhow, as he was a mile or so past the camp, the belt broke on his skidoo and he came to a stop. Most hunters have extra fan belts, and the man he borrowed the machine from was known for many things, but an extra of anything was not one of them.

Charlie was stuck. As nice of a day as it was, he knew he was the last hunter to make his way to the camp, and he was losing the light. As hard as he tried, he could not think of anything that would work. Then he remembered the camp.

So he decided to walk. It took a long time to get there and he used his skidoo trail as a path. He knew not to run, not to overheat. He took his time. Oh, I miss his walk. He was so handsome and he looked so relaxed all the time.

He made his way to the camp and knocked once before open-ing the tent flap to go in. Inside were several Inuit hunters. There was tea, he said. Pilot biscuits. No muktuk, but they had broth from seals.

He said hello and the hunters said hello back. Charlie explained his situation and the hunters listened to his Inuktitut.

The leader invited him in. "Eat," he said. And they served him. The hunters all had their guns and their harpoons. They had a little lamp of stone that they burned seal oil on. Charlie ate. It was so good to be home. Strangely, all of the men used *ulus,* the curved knife of the Inuit that looks like a quarter moon. Mom said the *ulu* was only for women and boys with girls' names.

"How do you know our language?" the leader asked him. "You have an accent."

"Oh," Charlie explained. He told them who his mother was and how he spent time in the west with his father. He apologized for speaking Inuktitut like a *kalunat.* A white man. And they all laughed.

"We do not know your mother," one of the hunters said.

"No?" Charlie asked. "She's a leader. She's helping get Nunavut off the ground. You must have heard of her."

The hunters all looked at each other. "No," they said. "Where are you going?"

Charlie gave them the name of a great hunter who was expecting him. He was surprised when the hunters all said they did not know of him or who he was. The man he was to join was famous for leading many community hunts and for fighting for the rights of hunters.

"Where have you come from?" they asked. "Have you seen any caribou?" He had come from Lypa's, his mom's boyfriend. He'd come right from the airport to Lypa's to get his gear, gun and skidoo and directions to the camp.

"We don't know him either," the leader said.

"Lypa?" Charlie said. "Everyone knows Lypa. He's a great carver. He's one of the trainers for the Canadian military with the Rangers."

Again, the hunters all looked at one another. "We do not know him either."

Charlie told me he had had a bad feeling, that he was a stranger to these people and that he had better leave. He explained to the hunters that the day was losing its light and that perhaps he'd better get back to his machine. He asked them if any of them had an extra belt, but they all said no.

"Then I'd better get going," he said. And he stood up to leave. He told me how he wished he'd had his gun then. It was the strangest feeling to think this amongst hunters, but he had it loud in his head to leave right away. That was when the leader touched his own rifle by his side and told him to sit down and keep talking.

"Why?" Charlie asked. "I am sorry, but it seems I have offended you somehow and I apologize. I am sorry you don't know my mother or the hunter who I am seeking or my mother's boyfriend."

"Keep talking," another hunter said who touched *his* rifle. Charlie stood again and the hunters all told him to sit.

"What is it?" Charlie said. "What have I done? I do not understand why you're treating me this way."

The leader held his hand up and motioned for Charlie to sit. "Keep talking," he ordered. "Prove to us you are not a white caribou."

Oh no! Charlie thought. He had heard for years about the white caribou. They are beings who pretend to be human and steal into camps pretending to be visitors, only to learn where the men are going to hunt the caribou. When they leave, they leave nothing but bad luck and afterwards the caribou are never where they're supposed to be.

"Prove to us you are human," the eldest hunter said. "Keep talking."

My Charlie sat, and he told me he spoke for what seemed like days. Days and days. They fed him and watched him. They questioned him over and over, the stories he told. He told them everything he could think of about his life and they listened carefully. When he was tired, they would let him sleep. When he had to use the bathroom, they went out with him. Sometimes it was day; sometimes it was night. It was then that he realized they had no dog teams, nor did they have skidoos. When he tried asking them questions, he was bullied to keep answering, to keep talking. Finally, after he burst into tears from exhaustion and after they'd all run out of food, the hunters let him go. He said he ran all the way back in the direction of town where the Rangers were looking for him.

My Charlie told that secret to me only because I nagged him and only because he loved me. I want you to know this.

And you know, I think it was that story that broke us. After that, everything fell apart. Bad luck found our home. Worse luck found our love. Charlie hurt his back; he couldn't work. He got mean. He was jealous when I came home happy. He told me he could not taste his food. We tried all we could to make things last, but I lost him. You know I lost him.

They say we live many lives in this one and we have to give thanks for our exes. I think about him more and more. Yes, I'm with Hank. Yes, our kids have grown. Yes, I have a home filled with memories of feasts and laughter. But then I heard that Charlie had gone missing. I heard he was training with the Rangers and that they were jogging and he vanished like he did—his footprints vanished—I knew because it was a raven who came to him the day his mother died. She had returned as a raven to say goodbye. That raven outside my window was Charlie telling me something I figured out some time ago.

The more I think about that story…. I figured it out. I figured *you* out. You see, that camp he described—there were no dogs. No skidoos. "Men" using *ulus*. And those hunters. How they treated him. How *you* treated him.

I think *they* were the white caribou. I think you are the white caribou. I think you were getting ready to split up and go after the camps and learn the plans of the hunters. I think he surprised you and that you made him earn his freedom as a human.

You know, he used to hold me in his sleep like a vice. Sometimes he'd shiver and yell out, "They're coming for me! They are, Susan. They're coming!"

I believe you came back for him. All of you. I believe you let him and his glorious heart go so he could live a few years and that you'd come for him so you could steal him back. I believe you missed him just as much as I do... all these years later. I think you know I know now. I think you know he told one person on this earth the story of all of you.

They say my family has medicine. It's true my grandmother saved her cousin from having his leg cut off due to diabetes using beaver castors. Ehtsi cured my styes using skunk juice. It's true she knows how to cure asthma. And she trained me how.

I was the one who told Charlie how to gather medicine under the full moon: to always work in fours; to always offer tobacco first; to talk to the earth and sky and spirit of the leaf, root or tree about why you were taking what you were from them. I tried passing this on to my kids and my husband but it never took. So I'm willing to pass it on to you. All I know. For your people.

I think you should come back and take me. When I think of how hard Charlie's life has been. When I think of his good heart, even when he was drinking. It wasn't his fault he told me the story about you. I was the one who figured this story out.

I've lived a good life. My kids are grown. My husband is a good man but he'll move on....

I have only been in love once in my life. I will tell you that. When I light this letter on fire and give it back to the spirit world... give my words back to the Creator and to you, I know you will see this letter and wish from the other side.

I will never tell anyone about you, and I have learned where the hunters are coming this month to find you. I've made my rounds in my own quiet way, and I will tell you everything. This is a good trade. I want you to consider my offer. I want you to consider this—

Lizard People

AND SO I HAVE THESE FRIENDS, GOD, WHERE DO I EVEN BEGIN? I have to set this up properly because I want to... I want to astound you. This is the craziest story you're going to hear today. All right? So I've got these friends and their names are Marvin and Stacy and they live in Vancouver, and Marvin is a man of many strong opinions. And we met them walking on the beach one night and we asked Marvin to take our picture and with a flick of his wrist, he created a timeless portrait, and we've been good friends ever since. So I was in Vancouver a while ago for business, and they are obsessed with David Icke, the writer and theorist and conspiracy buff.

And, I don't know if you know this, David Icke is convinced that there are Lizard People who live on the planet who have infiltrated our species and they're gearing up for a big strike. And so they're the reason that they put so many hormones in our milk because they're creating a new species of us — like a third sex (men with boobs, women with mustaches) — because they want to keep us weak and docile so that when the invasion comes, none of us will have weapons; all of us will have boobs and beards and there's nothing we can do. We're either going to make good pets or great food and it's up to them, right? It really is.

So that's the conspiracy. There's also the theory that with the chemical trails, every time a plane flies over a community, the chemical trails that we see from their engines are dropping a thin mist that the Lizard People have created and when doctors inoculate us, there is a sleeping agent in our blood streams that's activated and increases passivity in us all, so things have been set in motion and if you look at the US one-dollar bill, and you check out the pyramid, and you see that little eye in the pyramid, if you look carefully, it's actually a reptilian eye. And it's because the people who were engraving it were trying to warn us that the Lizard People are upon us. They're already here. But those people that had anything to do with that… they're all dead. Like, they died mysteriously as soon as that dollar was out. You need to look into this. Yes, you. All of you.

So, anyways, I'm in Vancouver, and I'm feeling really good about myself, and we go out for supper the night before, and they're telling us about how David Icke was in Vancouver and he has more evidence that Lizard People are here and they can prove it. And I'm like, "Well, okay, what's the story?"

And Marvin says, "Well, Stacy says that they have proof. This was in the paper. There was a lady in Vancouver who met a very handsome man and they were at the bar and they're drinkin' and so they ended up at her place and they start fooling around. And he has a hard body, a little eight-pack, eh? So they're fooling around; he's on top of her, and he's giving her the J strokes and he's plums-deep and things are great, and he feels fantastic and she's just running her hands along his side, you know, just feeling his lats, eh? And so what happened was, as he started to pick up the speed, she tried, like, grabbing his bum. Because you know when women are close, they like to hold on, eh? And what happened was, as she went to go grab his bum, something kept slapping her hand away. So she kept trying to get closer and closer to latch on cuz she was getting close now, and you know how when you're close with your woman and you want to ride that storm out together, like two horses lost in a wind storm but suddenly you find a way together by riding each other out, she just wanted to grab on, eh? Just let go with him, you know when the J strokes turn into the vinegar strokes, hey? But this little thing kept slapping her hands away from his bum, and what it was, was he had a tail. And the tail didn't want her to hold his bum. Yes! And so she let out this huge scream and from there, he pounced off the bed and he started running sideways along the wall. She saw his little tail and a flash of his eyes, and he had red eyes. He had reptilian eyes that GLOWED AT HER BECAUSE SHE KNEW NOW WHAT HE REALLY WAS! And that's how she knows that there's Lizard People—in Vancouver, no less."

And so they tell me that story and they're just looking at me for a reaction, and I'd just came back from Bali so I was no stranger to geckos, eh? I said, "Couldn't you imagine if when she screamed, she clenched, and his little peeny popped right off and was wiggling inside of her, like a little flipper? Can you imagine that?" And they were horrified that I suggested that because it just never crossed their minds.

So when you think of that story, you think of, like, the Lizard People, and I always think, "Well, why not?" Because we have Little People stories, we have White Caribou stories, we have the stories of the Deer Lady—the lady who's hitchhiking and when you look at her feet, under her jacket, she has doe's hooves—when you think about these shape-shifters, right, like, you've got the Wheetago and the Rougarou, the Loupgaroo, the Métis shape-shifting spirit—when you think of all these shifters, it makes me really happy to hear these stories, because I think that whether or not the Lizard People are here in actuality, it doesn't matter, right? Perhaps they are; perhaps they're not. It's good that people are telling these stories. Many of us have lost community and it makes me happy that these stories are being told. Whether it's around a supper table, in an elevator or around the water cooler. These are good stories and stories are how we grow as a people and family together.

A ho. A ho.

Godless but Loyal to Heaven

OH THESE PILLS ARE KICKING THE SHIT OUT OF ME... AND I COULD tell this was going to be about as much fun as a gut full of pinworms.

Jeezus, why me?

As I walked up the parking lot towards the hospital, there stood the Smith Squad chain-smoking outside the hospital doors. They stood straighter when I approached and they watched me cautiously. The Smith Squad was Lester's co-workers, guys who were all from Fort Smith, who worked for Jeremiah the Bullfrog. And there was Jeremiah's son and UFC hopeful: Country, the biggest boy in town. I don't know if it was a glandular problem or genetics or what the fuck, but he was a giant at easily six foot eight and solid with muscle. Because of his father's nickname, Townies called Country "Pollywog" as an act of irony, though never to his face. All of the men, including Jeremiah, stood in their overalls with their gloves off. I saw yellow trigger fingers on all of them from their smoking and I could tell they wanted to emanate criminal intent. They sipped coffee from Styrofoam cups and smoked, waiting to see what Jeremiah would do as I passed by. He said something quickly and Country pushed his chest up and walked out towards me.

I walked straight up to him and swallowed hard. My fists were all out of fights for me. *Think like a wolf....*

Gunner walked forward and stood beside Country, barring me from the door. He had no teeth so he looked a lot older than he was. Sharp knuckles. He spoke with his lips. Gunner probably blubbered to his pals that I jumped him, but that wasn't true at all. Of all my knockouts, he was my fave. I marvelled at how his spit flew and his ears wobbled every time I whooped him.

Gunner was the one who called me at Snowbird's and I could hear in his voice how much he hated me. I made a quick move towards him and Country and they both stepped back. I then looked at Jeremiah. "Fuck around," I said. "If Lester's dying and he's asked to see me, you're all in the way of a dying man's request."

I didn't really know the other members of the Smith Squad, except for Country, and I did not want anything to do with him—not with the body I had now. The other men were simple folk really, a wild assortment of the rough and ruthless and the tough and tooth-less—and then I sensed a great presence at three o'clock as the man in the back moved to oppose me while the others parted like weeds to let him approach.

I met his eyes, and he was a stranger. This was no Smither. He was Inuit from the east. The Inuk was short and stocky, powerfully built like Mike Tyson. He had long hair, a moustache and a little goatee. And nothing in his eyes for me but hate. He checked me out while the men snickered around me and I got the shiver, the same kind of shiver I felt when that daddy-long-legs spider ran across my ass the last time I used an outhouse. I knew, in a second, that this guy could really hurt me.

"Let 'im pass." Jeremiah leaned against the wall and stirred his coffee with the ass-end of a pencil. His voice was all Legion'd out and his canes leaned against him. "Lester's fadin' fast. We'd best respect that, eh, Torchy?"

The Inuk's eyes flashed to his left and there stood Jeremiah, the man the town nicknamed the Bullfrog, who was one of the Bay Boys who'd come up and never stopped running the north. The Bullfrog had worked out a sweetheart deal with the GNWT to hire the "worst of the worst" convicts and get them working for the town on day release. Everyone knew Jeremiah ran a tight ship and he fined his workers for the tiniest things. Chances were, if you worked for the Bullfrog, you were broke all the time, but you worked off your time faster than if you were in the pokey. "Nigger work" he called it, which didn't shock anybody coming from him.

The Inuk stepped back and I moved around him. The Inuk liked that a lot. In fact, as I passed him, he growled like a grizzly and the Smith Squad erupted in laughter. I did not want to tangle with this guy: I had a bad feeling about him and got the sense that with my TB fatigue, he had a few moves I couldn't get out of or break away from.

"Not yet," the Bullfrog said to the Inuk as if calming a bear with his voice, and I glanced at the Bullfrog's canes and black coffin shoes, as I always did, and made my way into the hospital. And I saw something else: the look Country gave his daddy was one of hurt and scorn—Jeremiah had a new favourite in his crew and his little Pollywog wasn't it.

Anyhow I could feel the gloom as soon as I walked down the halls and the first thing I smelled was a hot wave of piss and bleach. A sure sign that death was here to stay....

I walked down the hallway that Sfen painted a mural on. Of all the ones that he's painted around town, this is my favourite. On it, there are twenty-seven geese flying south. If you look at it closely, you can only see the geese. If you look at it from the spot where he painted two footsteps on the floor down the hall, you can see that the geese are the outline for an old woman with her braids blowing in the wind. It won him a lot of praise and even more contracts for logos and murals. Sfen chose twenty-seven because that's how hot it was the day I was born: twenty-seven degrees.

I touched the last one that signalled the tail end of her braid as I rounded the corner. "Hi, Sfen. My dearly departed brother."

The hallway outside Lester's room was filled with a few tables from the community centre that were packed with food, coffee, cookies, tea, bannock and apple juice with a pile of paper plates and cups for family and guests waiting together in round-the-clock shifts. Lester's room was the last on the wing, and I knew that this was where the hospital sent their terminal cases. It was here that they sent my mom when she decided to drink herself into the grave, and it would have served Sfen had he toughed it out. It looked like Lester's family and friends had been camped there for a while. There was a bunch of sad lookin' Natives in the hallway. I made my way to his room. His Auntie Sally wept into her hands, her hair hung over her face. I quickened my pace. *Shit. Was Lester already dead?*

Sally wiped her eyes and pointed to the open door. I knocked, and his uncle waved me in. It was dark in the room, so I made my way in. I smelled the cancer—sweet and high—before I saw him. And there he was: my first knockout and my greatest guilt. Lester.

As his uncle passed me and gave me a grim nod, the only things propping Lester's skeleton up were a lot of pillows. Lester barely had his head up with his eyes open. He looked green, like he hadn't seen sunlight in years. He had this pained look on his skinny face, and my legs ached as they always do when I see suffering.

Lester's mom was sitting next to him holding a Bible. There were Dene elders perched in their chairs all around the room. One lady was knitting and they all looked beat. There was no hope left in anyone's eyes. There was a lone candle burning in the room. It was scented and smelled of berries, probably to cover the smell of Lester being eaten alive from the inside. Although the room could hold two—maybe three—patients, the hospital had given the entire room to Lester and his family.

Lester's mom, Vivian, called me over and whispered, "My boy doesn't have long. He keeps asking for you." She motioned for everyone to clear out of the room and they did, but not before they all took turns giving me the evil eye. Maybe they knew.

Maybe they knew that I was responsible for Lester being the way he was, for not having as bright a life as he deserved. I never figured out why he ended up working for the Bullfrog: digging ditches, tarring roofs, replacing shingles, putting up Christmas lights on the power poles, because he wasn't a convict. He didn't have a mean bone inside of him. He was just simple, had seizures, is all. The room fell quiet and I looked around. Lester had a pile of tubes out his nose and wrists.

"Lester," I said quietly. His eyes flickered a bit.

I spoke a little louder. "Lester, it's me. Torchy."

There was another flicker. Lester was skin and bones, man. *Rough.* I covered my nose so I wouldn't smell him and looked away. *What the hell was he holding on for?* I wondered.

Lester was quiet, too quiet, and I wondered if he was already dead. I started thinking about leaving when he started to whisper. "Torch...."

I had to lean in close. I took off my jean jacket and pulled a chair up to his bed. "I'm here, buddy," I said.

"Torchy," he whispered. "You alone?"

I nodded. "Yeah. Everyone's gone."

He started to smile. "Thanks for coming."

"Sorry," I said. "I'm sorry this is happening."

"Not scared," he swallowed. "I'm not scared." His chapped lips were so dry; his skin looked like paper.

"Priest told me not to be afraid." Lester slowly reached up and touched the gold cross he had on a chain around his neck. "There's no pain where I'm goin'."

I nodded. "That's good."

He nodded, caressed the cross with his finger and tried smiling. "Heard you're a dad now."

I looked at him. "Yeah, sort of."

He then drifted off to sleep. I watched him and looked at all the gear they'd had him hooked up to. How on earth anyone could look after any or all of these machines and wires was beyond me. I remembered that Lester's family was Mountain Dene from Tulita. The thing about the Mountain Dene was when someone died, their tradition was to keep one thing of theirs and to burn the rest. Lester's head started to drop to the left when he jerked suddenly and said, "I wish I had kids." I started to breathe through my mouth.

His eyes fluttered under his eyelids. "Heard you're helpin' Snowbird out."

"Yeah," I said. "The old man needs help."

Lester quit smiling. He went still, quiet. I couldn't let him though. I hated the silence that started to fill the room like diesel fumes. Something told me I had to move fast before he slipped away. "What's up?" I asked. "What can I do to help?"

"He cured my cousin," Lester said.

That got me. "What?"

"Too bad he couldn't see me, but it's too late, I guess." I looked at him, swallowed, and said nothing.

"I need you to do two things for me," he said. "Can you?" I thought about it. *Shit.* I didn't need this. I needed money for grub. I was broke, had maybe five bucks and change to my name.

"Torchy?" he called again.

"Yeah," I said. "Still here. What do you need?"

"Did they tell you what I have?" he asked.

"No," I bluffed.

"Cancer of the heart," he said.

I hadn't heard that. I had just heard it was cancer. "I didn't even know you could get that," I said.

"Me, too," he whispered. "I got it. Full-blown. I know where I got it too, and I need your help."

"Go on, buddy," I sighed. "What can I do to help out?"

"Big meeting today," he said. "Town hall."

I'd heard something about it on the radio: mayor announcing that a bunch of prospective homeowners from across Canada were considering moving to town, and that we were to all extend the glad hand and welcome them here.

Lester swallowed hard and let out a loud burp. I sat up and moved back. "Sorry. It's the… pills. The town bought all these people one-way tickets to check out Simmer. The deal is if you buy a house, the town buys the second ticket home to pack up and get back here."

"Pretty smart," I said.

He nodded but stopped smiling. "You gotta stop it."

"What?"

"The meeting. You gotta stop it."

"Why?"

"She's a death trap," he whispered.

"What is?"

"The new subdivision. She's contaminated."

"With what?"

He got ready to burp again and I prayed he wouldn't vomit. He let out a moan and tried looking left towards the small table by the bed. "There any ice left?"

I was shocked. It was summer. Did he think it was winter? "You mean on the river?"

"In my cup," he whispered. "Did my mom leave some?"

I looked around and, sure enough, there was a Dixie cup filled with ice. Most of it was water, but there were a few ice chips.

"Please," he said, "run some ice along my lips." I picked up some ice. I wasn't crazy about it, but his lips were cracked to the point of looking plastic and split. I ran the ice cube along his lips and saw how handsome Lester used to be. Whoever had shaved him had missed a slice of stubble. There was a perfect triangle of hair under his chin down to his Adam's apple, which rose and fell as he slurped. His breath smelled sweet. Too sweet. There was that small golden cross on the chain and I shook my head: *there you go, again, God,* I thought. *Takin' a good kid too soon.*

Lester nodded he was okay. "It's going to kill my mom," he said. "Me dyin'."

"Come on now." I said. I looked around and saw pills, magazines, books of crossword puzzles and the air was thick, stale. "Got any chap stick?" I asked.

"Ice is better." He opened his eyes briefly but then shut them, letting out a pained moan. "Oh, the light hurts me, Torchy. My eyes hurt. Can you ask the old man to pray for me?"

I looked around and saw the Bible on the table beside his bed. What was the Bible verse Sister Regan always quoted to me and Sfen? Proverbs 4:14-16.

"Torchy?"

"Huh?"

"Can you ask Snowbird to pray for me?"

I nodded. "I will."

He seemed suddenly out of breath. "Candle's fine. I'm okay. I'm okay. Ask him to pray for my mom, too. I don't want to leave my mom." Then he faded.

I waited, looked around. "What's that land contaminated with?"

He spoke again: "Uranium. The government used Simmer as a transport route to the States."

I'd heard something about that. "Go on."

He started to wheeze a bit before going on. "We helped clear out that subdivision for the mayor. We found uranium rocks everywhere. They told us not to touch 'em. The Bullfrog got us to load them up in his dump truck late at night and move them somewhere. I heard 'em talkin' and I called Jeremiah on it that night. He told me to keep it hush hush, but there's still lots there. I know we didn't get it all. We couldn't have. I just know that's how I got this."

That made sense. The mayor was a pretty crafty dude. It was funny how any lucrative deals always had his name included in the fine print. "How many families are thinking of moving in?"

"There's enough lots... for twenty homes this year. They were aiming for... another twenty lots next year. It's where the old highway used to be. I told Jeremiah he should call someone, feds maybe, to clean 'er up."

"Uh huh. What'd he say?"

"He told me to mind my own business."

I shook my head. "Fucker."

He nodded. "The meeting's at three."

I realized what he was asking me to do. The big clock on the wall said it was 2:40. I started to shake my head. "I ain't no public speaker," I said.

"Please, Torchy. Think of those people. Think of the kids."

I thought of Stephanie. "What do you want me to say?"

"Grab that mike. No one will stop you. Tell those people no one can move there. You gotta do it or they'll all end up like me. Think of those kids. Imagine that girl of yours with cancer." I winced. "I don't know what I'd do if anyone suffered like me... even on the other side. I think I'd go to hell, Torch, if you don't do this. Please."

It made sense, what Lester said. Sfen had always called that part of town the "circle of death." It seemed that everyone on the north end of town—sooner or later—got cancer. We noticed it when we were in our teens. Some folks moved away and were okay, but the folks who stayed were always sick. It was sad. Pick up a copy of the paper and there was always a quiltin' bee for buddy's wife for her cancer or a prayer circle for another person. All of them lived in the "circle."

The new subdivision was a little west of there. I remembered trails in the bush when we'd go looking to torch-and-destroy forts. I always wondered why there were bush trails already cleared out. I guess it was for a road and it could be true that it was the road that ran through the circle of death and to an old transport route that led to the old highway.

"Torchy?" he asked.

"Yeah?"

"Will you do it?" My face burned. I couldn't answer.

"You said you'd defend me until my dying day, 'member?" I looked at Lester and couldn't believe it. I didn't think he'd ever heard me promise that, but he did.

Fuck sakes. Lester was askin' me to do something that I didn't want to do, nor could I picture doing, and yet I'd set out to help. But I didn't feel like walkin' up to a show-and-tell meeting about what a great town this was and telling the mayor off. I looked at Lester and saw that candle flicker. I just knew that this was the time to make my peace with him before he found his.

The candle flickered again — maybe from the wing flutter of spirit helpers waitin'. That's what Snowbird would say. I looked at Lester and thought, "There you go again, God, siccin' something cruel on a good man and eatin' him out from the inside until there's nothing left while the drunks stagger, the junkies endure and some Indian woman is gonna do the FAS dance on the bar floor in town tonight. If you love us so much, how come you brought cancer and AIDS and everything else down here?"

"Lester," I said. I swallowed hard. "Remember when we were kids?"

He nodded. "Yeah."

I took a big breath and decided to come clean. "Remember that day we were running towards the school and I kicked the door shut—"

"I know you're sorry," he said.

I looked at him. He was smiling. "How do you know what I was going to say?"

"Because every time you drink you call my house saying how sorry you are."

I thought about it. Was he joking? "What?"

"Nobody's got a voice like yours. It didn't take much to figure it was you."

I thought about it. I always wondered why I woke up on top of the phone after getting snaked out of shape. "What would I say?"

"You always said, 'Sorry for making you retarded.'"

I burst out laughing. "No way. I didn't say that."

He let out a long breath and winced. "You cry," he said. "You cry hard."

I looked down. *Holy shit.* It all made sense.

"You didn't make me the way I am," he said. I was quiet because he was wrong.

It was a Friday and the sun was shining. I guess you could say I was a bully and Lester was my favourite score. I never close-fisted him or nothing. I'd just push him around and slap him sometimes until he quit lookin' so happy.

We were in grade seven and he and I were racing for the door. Okay, I admit: I loved roughing him up until he cried. I never took his money or his lunch—well, sometimes—but I wasn't happy until he was crying. He always had nice clothes and good food. You could just tell he had a home filled with love. I hated the fact that he could read and write better than me. I just knew that while I was going without, his parents were reading him to sleep. Lester was a fast little fucker and was just giving 'er, boy, towards the door. He knew if he could get into the school, he was home free. It was one of those things where nothing is spoken but you both know that you got to get to that door or the world will explode. I knew about ten paces in that he was going to beat me, so I got this bright idea that if I drop-kicked the door shut with all my might, I'd cut him off and I could beat him up for running from me. So I launched into the air and stomp-kicked that door, but his head got in the way. I kicked that door, and that goddamned heavy fire door, it slammed into his head. And I kicked with everything I had—and I knocked him cold.

I can still hear that door slamming on his skull. Lester went into convulsions and was gurgling all over the place, and we were the only ones there. I was so scared I didn't know what to do. If I ran for help, I'd get in trouble, expelled for sure. I panicked and didn't do a thing. I just watched him twitch and make those horrible sounds, "Nggg nggga nggggaaahhhh," and I thought I finished him and that these were his death kicks.

I knew enough to turn him on his side so that his mouth could empty and I waited it out with him, eyeing the door so no one saw. If anyone discovered us, I was gonna play the hero, say I found him like this, but nobody came. Payday, I guess. Everyone was home.

What scared me most were his eyes. They were like the eyes of a stunned jackfish.

I waited him out and he just lay there, and that's when I got on my hands and knees and told him to breathe. I reminded him to breathe because he wasn't. I couldn't hear it. I was like, "Holy fuck, Lester! Breathe. Breathe. Come on, buddy. You can do it. I swear to God, Lester. If you make it I will never beat you up again. Come on, buddy," I was lookin' around. "You can do it. Lester, I am so fucking sorry. I swear to God that I will defend you until your dying day. I will kill anyone who crosses you, buddy. I swear —Lester!"

Well, he made it. He came to and I held him, man. I held him like a fuckin' meat puppet. I was rocking him and telling him to breathe. I took my sock off and wiped his spit and guck from his boiling mouth away, and I held him. And I prayed. Let me tell you, I fucking prayed for the first time in my life. I made a deal with God to make him okay, to not kill him. I prayed, boy, until I meant it.

But, you know, God double-crossed me again: Lester never really did come back. Soon after, Lester started to have the boiling mouth and seizures. All the time. He'd drop in the hallway, or downtown, or even when we were writing our finals, and I kicked the shit out of every kid who made fun of him. Lord knows that's where I learned to down the toughest kids in school. I tracked down every one of them and I fought them all. Pretty soon, every time Lester dropped, kids would run for help or move everything out of his way or turn Lester on his side—even get the muck out of his mouth—because we'd *all* done our homework.

But all the while, I felt like shit. I had done this to him. I had ruined him for life. It was my fault. Little Lester with the shiny hair every day because he had good shampoo from the drug store, little Lester who had ColecoVision while I had only fuckin' CBC, Little Lester who had all the Star Wars figures while I got slapped for bawling on Christmas when I asked how come we didn't even have a tree.

"Leave him alone," Sfen would tell me. "He didn't do anything to you."

"Fuck you," I snapped. "He's laughing at me." But the truth was Lester smiled all the time because he was a happy person, and I wasn't. God had a plan for him while he'd forgotten me.

And the horror show didn't end there. Lester had to be moved to the Special Program where he had a specialized tutor. He never got his matriculation diploma; he only got his general — and that was basically a freebie because everyone knew he was fucked for life. *Ah shit*, no one knows how many years I grieved for what I'd done. I felt so bad. I'd go out of my way to be super nice to him. I dug his mom out of the ditch one winter and refused payment. One time I gave him a lift home in a snowstorm and we didn't say a word all the way home.

I looked at him and said, "I didn't think you heard me."

"I heard you," he smiled. "It's not your fault."

I looked at my hands. "I gave you seizures."

He shook his head once. "I had epilepsy before you ever did that to me."

I sat up. *"What?"*

"I had a few seizures before you ever did that."

"Come on," I said. "I couldn't have helped."

"No," he smiled. "That couldn't have helped."

I said. "Lester, I want you to know I never beat on anyone who didn't deserve it after that."

"Why?" he asked. "I always wanted to know why you were so mean to me." I thought about it. My natural urge was to lie, but I fig- ured: *why lie to the dying? Why not let 'em know the truth?* Snowbird once said that sometimes people die because they can do more as a spirit than they ever could alive.

I bit the bullet and told the truth: "Because you had it all, man. You got everything I ever wanted. You had it made."

He nodded. "It's not your fault."

I hung my head and confessed, "I was always worried I killed the best part of you."

He reached out and touched my arm. I flinched. I don't like to be touched. "You never wrecked me," he said and rested his hand on my arm. "I promise you never did."

I relaxed my arm and let him rest his hand there. I thought about his request and thought, *ah fuck it, I'm broke but not broken*. I may have had TB in my blood but I could do this. "Okay." I took a big breath. "I'll do 'er. I'll tell the folks to not move there."

He nodded and squeezed my hand. "One more thing."

I hung my head. Shit. He was dying right in front of me. "What?"

"I got a secret."

I looked at him. Hadn't this just been one?

"Son?" a voice called behind me. It was his mom. I don't know how long she'd been there. "Are you okay?"

"I'm okay, Mom. Just about finished. Is there any more ice?"

And that's when he started talking. He told me a story that blew me away. With tubes breathing for him and keeping him alive, he told me his biggest secret and woke me up to his secret life. As he spoke, he filled me with his *inkwo*, his medicine, his hope, and I felt strong. For the first time in weeks, I felt strong. We were only interrupted once and that was by his uncle. I guess by the look in my eyes, he knew I was being called into service and he left us alone. When he was done and as he drifted off, I rose quietly and left without saying a word to anyone. I knew what I had to do.

I walked into that meeting at town hall and there was a sea of local and tourist faces all sweating away. The mayor had pulled the same trick his father pulled and his father before him: they cranked the heat up an hour before the meeting so people would either fall asleep or want things over fast. It was no surprise that the Bullfrog was there without his men. How pathetic. He probably didn't want them learning that they could all die like Lester by handling the uranium.

Jeremiah wasn't too happy I was there and shook his head when he saw me walk in. I could tell by his eyes that he knew I knew about the little subdivision cover up. He knew that Lester had told me everything, and that's probably why he was at the hospital. It wasn't to say goodbye to his best worker; it was to see who Lester 'fessed up to.

It was then that I had a little flashback to when we were kids. Jeremiah used to own the only gas station in town. One day, me, Mom and Sfen were on the way to Hay River for a road trip with her boyfriend. Sfen and I needed to use the bathroom before we hit the highway.

The town had already targeted Sfen as being gay, so I never let Sfen go anywhere without me. When we asked for the keys to the bathroom, the Bullfrog gave Sfen the key to the women's room. I saw Sfen's cheeks burn in shame.

"What's this?" I asked.

"Other one's broken," Jeremiah grinned.

I looked at the men's room and there was no sign on it saying it was broken. "Bullshit," I said. I remember this was the one week when Sfen and I were considering being priests. I remember in catechism the nun would ask, "Who made you?"

"God!" we'd cheer.

"Why?"

"To make us better Christians!"

"Why?"

"To bear the name of Jesus!"

I felt so good around the nuns and priests. There were no questions, no judgment. I felt clean. Sfen did, too. It was our secret and we'd only told one nun about our wish and she was delighted. But it was shit like this that took us back to the real world, and I wasn't letting anyone pick on Sfen.

"You don't like it you can go outside," the Bullfrog grinned. "Plenty of pansies to piss on, you know?" He gritted his teeth when he said this and there was an edge to his voice that ignited the fury gene.

Sfen hung his head and started to walk towards the exit. I saw his eyes and they were just brimming with tears. *Fuck this,* I thought. There was no one around so I whipped out my unit and started peeing in the store. Jeremiah was astonished. He started fumbling with his canes going, "Hey! Hey!" When he came around the counter to get me I started peeing in that direction, and all the while I heard laughter coming from Sfen.

My piss was running out and I could tell Jeremiah was going to charge with his canes, so I let him know in no uncertain terms that if he fucked with us we'd burn his house down, and he seen my snake eyes so he knew it was true.

"If you ever pull that shit again with my brother," I said, "you'll lose more than your house and you know it."

We'd already burnt down the old residential school but we were too young to go to jail. Young Offenders, hey.

"Get the fuck out of my store," he spat.

I nodded. "Let's go, brother."

And we strolled back to the car smiling.

"How's your father, Torchy?" Jeremiah called from behind me.

I froze. Turning around, I could see him leaning outside the door. "Father's Day is coming up. You gonna call him or get him a present?"

My blood turned to gasoline. *What did he know that I didn't?*

"Torchy," Sfen called. "What is it?"

I didn't know, but something felt wrong.

The Bullfrog called out even louder. "You better go to the drugstore and get your daddy something cuz he sure loved your mother, boy. Oh did he ever."

I glanced and Mom and Rob didn't hear anything. They had the radio cranked and the windows were closed.

I charged with all I had and he closed the door before I got there. I heard the Bullfrog bolt it and I tried everything I could. "Your dad raped your mom, Torchy," he said through the barred windows. "You were born a bastard and you'll die a bastard. You'll never be anything different." I was stunned. I froze and looked at him without knowing what to do. It was true that Sfen and I looked different. I was darker than he was. We had different coloured eyes. He looked half white. I looked nothing but Indian.

I swung my head his way and looked for something to destroy. He was lucky I couldn't get at him that day. His truck was locked. The pumps were locked. There were bars on all the windows. He knew something about my dad and I could tell what he said was true. Jeremiah the Bullfrog had made a fortune by using people's worst secrets and greatest shames against them.

All he had made me was a sworn enemy.

"It's okay, Torchy," Sfen said, patting my shoulders. "It's okay."

"What is it?" Mom asked.

"Nothin'," I shrugged as the hot tears started to flow.

"Think like a wolf," Sfen whispered and I nodded. I knew not to rock the boat when Rob was around so I decided to bide my time and ask Mom when we were all alone. *Who was my dad?*

I listened to the mayor and thought, *you cocksucker.* He had the plans for the new subdivision, but he didn't mention the circle of death or that we had the highest rate of cancer in the western NWT. He talked about how we had the lowest land taxes in the Northwest Territories, and he talked about what the town had to offer, but he didn't talk about the cancer or the leukemia or the sickness that stalked the home-owners in the north end of town, and how the cancer that walked there was just aching to meet them, starving to feed on them and their kids.

One man asked why the new subdivision was the only place that was available to build and develop. "What if I find land elsewhere for my family?"

The mayor talked about how the new subdivision was the only place in town you could build because of the land claims that were up in the air with the Cree. There was a land freeze goin' on, he explained, but that would settle itself over the next few years.

I watched him, really watched his eyes. The mayor was so good at lying you could never tell that he was condemning you to cancer and leukemia. He then opened up the mike to the public and that's when I walked forward.

It was something seeing those new faces in town. Lord knows we needed some new DNA in the gene pool. We were all starting to look a little too much alike and there was one hot-looking wife who would have spruced things up in town if she and her hubby chose to live here.

As I walked towards that mike, the mayor stopped smiling. He was surprised that I had something to say. He'd tried to have me banished from town when my brother and I were younger, but he'd failed. The sentencing circle had kept me in town and he wasn't too happy about that.

"Yes, um," the mayor said, "one of our local, ah, men is going to speak."

He wouldn't say my name. I looked around at oh roughly thirty people. There were a few contractors standing by the coffee machine. There was the manager of the drugstore and the manager of the Northern standing by. Anyone who had anything to gain from the new blood that would be moving to town was here and they looked worried that I was getting ready to speak. The rest of the people—the southerners—all looked at me with smiles.

"Oh, what trusting eyes," I whispered into the mike. "I can't lie to you today." I gripped that mike and looked to the crowd. "Ladies and gentlemen, my name is Torchy and I am here to tell you that you're walking into a death trap. You and your families." The room gasped and everyone sat up. I then turned and pointed at him. "Fuck you, Mister Mayor," I said. "Fuck you and your lies." He gave me the dirtiest look and made a move towards me but stopped when he saw the reporter for the newspaper start snapping pictures.

"Many of us here call that part of town where you all are thinking of moving 'the circle of death' for a reason. Do not move here if you intend on raising your families there. Do not believe anything this man has just told you. That whole new area is filled with uranium. There's a young man in town dying right now because of it."

And I spilled the beans. I spilled them hard. I told the folks why they couldn't move here and I told them about the uranium. I told them that the mayor knew there was probably uranium exactly where they would be building their homes. I did say that Simmer was the best place in the north to live — but not at Uranium Death Trap Central.

The mayor was fuming. I admit I enjoyed seeing him blush, and I dared him to stop me. There were no cops. There was nobody tough in the room that I couldn't handle. There was just the steady click of a reporter's camera in town going bananas. I dared either the mayor or the Bullfrog to even come close, but they were petrified into stillness the whole time I spoke.

Needless to say, nobody in that room was smiling when I finished. In fact, in my little five-minute speech, nobody was even looking at me. They were all turned to the mayor. The photographer from the local paper snapped a shot that would make the cover of next week's paper for sure.

"Thank you for listening," I said. "Would anyone else like to talk?" I didn't wait. I walked towards the door.

The Bullfrog's neck and jowls were actually purple. I wondered if he'd try and cane me, but all he did was crumple his coffee cup and throw it on the floor. "Sonofabitch!" he said. "That was a done deal, Torchy."

I stopped and looked at him. "Fuck off," I said. "You coulda killed all those people." I walked towards him, cocked the hammer and he backed up fast. "How'd you like chewing a fuckin' T-Bone steak every night for the rest of your life knowing that families were fuckin' dying because of where you built their homes?"

"You're dead, Torchy. We're gonna finish this off later." He fumed but made no aggressive motion towards me, so I dismissed him and moved on. I had to beeline it to the bar and finish my second task. I looked back once and nobody came after me. They all wanted a piece of the mayor and surrounded him like wolves.

Lester's second secret was what I had to contend with next, but he told me to call before I proceeded. I went to the phone booth by the four-way stop and fished around for my second-last quarter, found it and dropped 'er in before the switchboard at the hospital picked up and I asked for Lester.

"Can I ask who's calling?" the lady asked.

"A friend." I could see Sfen's logo for the Spirit Bear Sports Store in town. The logo was of two bears—one black and one brown—smiling and facing forward, as if cheering. They wore head-bands and jerseys and were holding hockey sticks. Of course, the jerseys both read "Spruce Kings" after our home team. This was the Disney phase in Sfen's work and the townies loved it. At the opening, Sfen said that the black and brown bears playing together represented harmony, but he told me that the brown bear was him and the black bear was me. I held my hand up and blocked out the bear that was me.

"I'm sorry, sir," the receptionist said, "but Lester's family has asked that only family—"

"Look," I said and dropped my hand. "I was just in there. Can you please put me through—"

"Is this Torchy?" she asked.

"Look, Lester asked me to—"

"I'm sorry, Torchy." And I knew....

"Lester just passed away a few minutes ago." My heart sank and I felt so suddenly tired.

"Fuck sakes," I said. "No—really?"

"I'm sorry... his mother would like to talk to—"

Fuck! I hung the phone up and walked away. I took a big breath and pictured that candle blowing itself out, and I pictured Lester smiling at me in his sleep as I left him. I'd done the first thing I promised for him, and I knew I had to do the last. Fuck!

For fuck sakes, God. How much innocent blood do you need today? What's your fuckin' misery quota?

I made my way towards the bar and it hit me: Did I even tell Lester I was sorry? I thought of his last words to me. "I don't want to go to hell, Torchy. Promise you'll help me not go to hell."

And I thought of my last words to him. "You ain't going to hell," I said. "I promise you."

Ah fuck. I swayed as I walked and thought, "You can trust pain in this life, and that's about it." I thought of Lester and his spirit, probably taking a walk beside me to make sure I'd keep my promise. "You ain't going to hell, Lester. I did what you asked. And I'm sorry about being so mean to you when you were a kid. I'm about to complete the mission you gave me. Hey, if you see Sfen, tell him I love him, okay?"

The Terminal was not a place I enjoyed going into, especially not today. Imagine walking into a nest of your worst enemies who have had the luxury of powering up for the past six months while you've only grown weaker.

I know Stephanie felt bad for bringing TB my way, but I told her I needed to lose the weight. Fuck, I hate being weak.

"Are these vitamins?" she asked me one day when she found Sfen's meds still in the fridge. She was holding them like candy.

"They were supposed to be," I said. "For my brother."

She put them back and I made her wash her hands. It was funny. I had cleaned out just about everything but I just couldn't bring myself to throw all of his pills away. Not yet. I'd boxed up his clothes—well, most of them, and I wore this shirt, his favourite shirt, but why couldn't I burn those fuckin' useless pills or his shirt or his clothes? And there was his Bible on his nightstand by his bed. I didn't know what to do with it. The strength would leave me even just thinking about it.

I decided to call the old man from the lounge. The bar band had taken a break before the jukebox turned on and it was quiet enough for me to dial. The old man picked up on the third ring. "Hello?"

"Hey," I said. "How's baby girl?"

"Nosy," he said. I smiled. It was Friday. Stephanie's aunt had to work on Fridays so we took turns looking after her if Auntie Freda's babysitter situation fell through. "What's going on over there?"

"We're visiting. How's your friend?"

I felt my breath leave my body with the sad news. "Didn't make 'er."

"Sorry to hear that. I'll drop some tobacco for him on his way."

"Hey," I said. "I didn't want to say it in front of Steph but I'm broke. If I find some money I'll be home by six with grub."

"Ho," he said. "We got chicken, spuds, Niblets. I think we'll be okay. My pension cheque comes in on Friday."

It was Wednesday. We could stretch what we had, but I'd need a few hours to set this up. "If I'm late, don't worry. Lester had a last request."

"Then that's where you need to be," he said. "Oh. Just wait. Someone else wants to talk." I could hear him in the background telling Stephanie not to be so bossy.

"Hello?"

I tried to smile but suddenly felt so incredibly tired. "Hi, Stephanie. How are you?"

"Do you know where my Goofy toothbrush is?"

"Ah," I thought. I bought Steph a toothbrush with Goofy on it. "Maybe at Sfen's?"

"Can you bring it if you go there?"

"Sure."

"When are you coming home? I'm already done colouring your pictures."

"Already? Get Snowbird to draw you something."

"Hellooo. News flash. He's blind?"

"I see more than you," I heard the old man say and they started laughing.

"I'll be home soon," I said. "I have to do a favour for my friend."
"Is he okay?"
"I'm afraid not, baby girl. He's pretty sick."
"I'm sorry I made you sick."

The duo I had been sent to track walked into the bar. This was going to be easy. I could say what Lester wanted me to say and then I could go home for supper. "It's okay. I'll be home later. Take care of Grandpa, hey?"

"Cuddles says hurry home so we can do the monkey dance!" She started laughing, and I could hear Snowbird telling her to help him peel potatoes. For a blind man, Snowbird was actually quite the chef.

"Bye!" she said and hung up.

I looked at the phone and shook my head. *Cuddles says hurry home, no less....* With Stephanie came a cat. Cuddles. I'm so allergic to that cat it's not even funny, but oh well. The monkey dance was something Stephanie started when she felt better about leaving her mom. She asked me one day to impersonate a monkey walking. Snowbird was in the next room. I don't know... I can't say no to her. So there I was, wiggling around the room with my arms up like an orangutan walking in circles going, "Oo Oo Oo!" and she killed herself laughing. I hadn't heard a laugh so fun since forever so I kept doing it. Snowbird came into the room and kept asking, "What's so funny?"

Which made me laugh. Then I started walking around him in a circle and Stephanie started following me going, "Oo Oo!" and Snowbird kept reaching out going, "Hey now. What's so funny?"

So every night now, we do the Monkey Dance and it's become something we all look forward to. Snowbird just shakes his head and goes, "Boy, you guys..." but I can tell he's smiling when we do it.

I remembered when we went to the lake for a picnic: Stephanie, the old man and me and her auntie. We were up on a cliff, overlooking the stream. Suckers were running but I was too chicken to swim for fear one would bite me—even though they could only nibble. Stephanie swam with her aunt, and I cooked up a fine meal of hot dogs, beans and spuds. Stephanie liked eating beans cold—right from the can. Man, that was pitiful. Who likes cold beans?

The old man and I were keeping an eye—well, I was keeping an eye, the old man was keeping an ear, let's say—out for our girl and a wind picked up around us. It was funny because it was such a sunny day and yet this wind came up and it meant business. I had to grab some rocks to weigh down the bag of buns, plates and napkins. But there, in the wind, Snowbird and I sat in a warm spot. It was like the wind had circled around us, and couldn't reach us.

"You feel that?" I asked.

Snowbird nodded and crossed his legs, sitting up with his cane. "I get my answers here."

He said it so fast that I froze. I looked at the old man and he was not smiling at all. He was doing that thing where he listened. You could sense it. You could *feel* him listening with his blood.

That's when Snowbird looked at me and smiled. "I can see here."

I got spooked, so I busied myself and got back to work cooking. Funny thing about Snowbird was he started teaching me about the Dogribs. For the first time in my life, I started to understand more and more about my inheritance as a Tlicho. I remember one night I asked him, "Snowbird?"

"Hmm?" he turned to me.

"Can I ask you about the old times?"

He nodded. "What would you like to know?"

"How did we get around?"

"Snowshoes. Moosehide boat. Dog teams."

"Huh. Did we use teepees or make lean-tos?"

"Caribou-skin teepees."

"Take it easy," I said and lit a smoke. "We used teepees like the Crees?"

"We used teepees."

"What did we fight with before guns?"

"Medicine."

"What about guys like me, like without...."

"Bows, spears, knives."

"Knives of what?"

"Antler."

"Huh. What kind of arrows did we use?"

"Four kinds," he said. "One for fish, one for birds, one for small game, one for big game, like moose and men."

"Really?" I liked this. "And what were our arrowheads made out of?"

"Black glass."

"Take it easy."

"You take it easy," he said.

"Glass from where?"

"Rock," he said. Was there glass in rock? I had never seen any.

I nodded. "Tell me more." He made the motion of holding a bow on its side and firing from his hip.

"We shot our bows sideways, from our waist. Not like the Inuit or the Chipewyan. They fired standing up, arrow by their eye."

"How come we fired from our hips?"

"More accurate," he said. "You never miss if you know what you're doing."

"How did you know you had medicine?" This was something we had never really talked about before.

"Why?" he asked.

"I want to know, for the girl. She's starting to ask questions."

He nodded and moved his fake teeth around in his mouth when he thought. "Dogribs," he said. "By the time a baby is three, if the people thought the baby had medicine, they'd leave the baby out on the land."

I thought of Stephanie. "With what?"

He looked at me. "Nothing."

"Why?"

"You either walked out alive or you didn't." I couldn't believe it. I knew we were tough, but not that tough.

He nodded. "This way, when someone was known as a medicine man, they were respected. They had earned it."

"Did your parents do this to you?" I asked and winced.

His body tightened and he got out his pipe. "I never knew them. They died in the sickness."

I reached for a smoke. Sfen told me a bit about this. "TB? Influenza?"

"We never gave it a name. Sickness just kept coming. You had to keep moving." I nodded.

"And what about you?" he asked.

I looked up. "What about me?"

"I heard about you for years. You're a fighter."

I nodded, surprised at the old-timer. "It's true."

"What are you fighting for?"

I had never thought about it before. "I don't know."

"Peace maybe."

"What?"

"Maybe you're fighting for peace."

"Riddles, old man. You always speak in riddles."

And he smiled. "I'm not the one who lights fires."

"What?"

"I know your tricks. I always wanted to ask you why." He looked at me. "The girl wants to know. She's doing research."

I smiled. Snowbird was clever as a raven and ruthless as a wolverine. "My brother always told me that fire was how God cleaned."

Snowbird nodded. "Your brother was right. But the Dogribs have always used fire."

I got the tingles. "Why?"

"Epidemics. You know, they're settling land claims now."

"When was our treaty signed—1921?"

"Some signed under Treaty 8 in 1899. But don't forget: Dogribs signed four treaties in 1920. We were not interested in giving up any land. We took treaty to live in peace, not surrender."

I joked: "Were you there?"

He nodded. "I was."

"Old man, how old are you?"

He smiled. "I can't remember." I believed it. There was no one left alive who could remember Snowbird as a young man. He was remembered as always being ancient.

"The Dogrib copy of this agreement was burned when the people had to burn everything during the last epidemic. The other three copies have never been recovered."

"Really?" Sfen would have loved this information. I bet he could have found them all. "You say the Dogribs had to burn everything."

He nodded. "The people. They died so fast. You'd go on the land to trap for a few days and the people you waved goodbye to were dead when you got back. We had to burn everything."

I covered my eyes. Holy fuck! Maybe this was why I burned everything down. Tribal memory, I guess. "Who knows about this?"

He shrugged. "You and me."

"Snowbird," I said. "Thank you—*mahsi*." He nodded and held out his hand. I shook it, gently.

And in my dead brother's shirt, sitting in the Spruce Lounge surrounded by bar stars and denim queens, I said another quick prayer for Lester. "Sorry, buddy," I said. "I'm sorry you never made 'er. Say hi to my mom if you see her, too."

"What'll it be, Torchy?"

I looked and it was Thelma. Sweet and voluptuous Thelma. We used to go to school together and she had this smile on that I had never seen from her before. Well, maybe I saw it a few times.

I shook my head. "I'll be leaving fast."

"Oh no you don't," she said. "This one's on me."

"Oh?" I asked.

She nodded. "Yup. I see you every day when I'm having my morning coffee, piggybackin' that girl of yours, and I think that's just the sweetest thing. Is she your daughter?"

"Me?" I was surprised. "Well, we adopted each other as brother and sister, but yeah…she does feel like my daughter."

"That's sweet." She leaned forward and winked. "Want your usual?"

I smiled and my chest warmed from within. I was dying for a shot of prairie fire, but I didn't want the girl or the old man to smell it on me. "How about a big glass of ice with some Coke and a twist of lemon?"

"Good for you, Torchy. I'll be right back." I nodded and looked around. I thought of the night I somehow ended back at her place. This was about a year ago, I guess. She now owned the house I grew up in. I couldn't believe it. There we were. And the memories started flooding back in.

She'd done a good job with the new paint, nice pictures hung up, but you could still smell the fear, the smell of hope on fire, the fear we felt all the time growing up. I think humans give off a scent if they've lived in terror for years in a house that was never a home.

She gave me a tour and showed me her clothes room. I didn't have the heart to tell her that that was where Rob stored his guns. On a mattress. The same mattress he took me on and made me do things. It was either me or Sfen, he said. I got to choose. I let it be me out of love for my brother. Thelma showed me the basement and I could see the nail. *The Nail….*

That fucker would take me and Sfen down in the basement when we were bad and he'd make us kneel on all fours and smack the back of our heads into the head of The Nail and a hot hail of blood would rain on our hands.

"Are you scared of the basement?" he'd whisper. *"Are you scared?"*

That son of a bitch. The day I found out he'd gotten Sfen, too, I waited until he got good and drunk before destroying his face and dousing him with gasoline. Sfen was the only fuckin' thing that held me back.

"What is it?" she said and took my hand.

"Nothin'," I said.

"You're shaking."

I could feel blood pooling in my hands. "Naw."

"I want to get to know you, Torchy."

"No you don't."

She looked up at me. "I do."

"You have no idea what I am, do you?" I asked.

"No," she said. "But I want to." She leaned into me and I felt her heartbeat through her shirt.

"Are you afraid of the basement?" I asked.

"I never come down here," she said. "I don't like it." I closed my eyes and I felt her hands unclench my fists.

She rolled my shirt up so she could see the scars on my forearms. "What did these used to be?"

"Oh now," I said and looked away. "Let's not talk about sad things tonight." It took a whole night of dabbing myself with a red hot car lighter to smolder the letters outta me.

"You don't scare me, Torchy." I looked at her, into her kind eyes and put my battle stance away. She took my hand and led me upstairs. I looked in my old room and it was all cleaned up. Fresh paint. I saw a braid of sweetgrass on a dresser and pictures of her folks when they were younger in the bush.

"There was a bad spirit here," I said. "But you and your good heart—you made it go away."

I looked in the bathroom. Sfen and I used to bathe in the same tub, singing together. I looked in her room and saw a queen-sized bed.

"Come," she said and I did. Her long hair sweeping over me. Thelma's soft skin. All the hurt and rage I had she took away and she took all of me. Everything I had. And I came until there was nothing left but her fine glorious light.

We tried a few times to make a go of it but she told me she wanted kids and ah, well, fuck. Plus, some guy kept calling the house and hanging up and she'd get a look in her eyes. That look of longing. I could tell she had someone on the side so I quit coming around. But it was good to see her. It has always amazed me how beautiful most women are without their clothes on. Like, you'd never guess by looking at them with their clothes on that they are such goddesses underneath. Dressed? They're a six out of ten. Undressed they're like *Mama Mia!* She was like that. So womanly and soft. Sometimes I can still feel her bucking in my hands.

I looked around the Terminal but couldn't relax. It was like *Planet of the Apes* in there: Chipewyan, Cree, Mountain, Slavey, Gwich'in, whites, all at their miserable worst. A couple Inuit all gave me the stink eye. That drink couldn't come fast enough, and I couldn't wait to seal the deal with Lester, but Charity and Vincent were sure taking their sweet-ass time. Where were they? Probably dealing in the staff room with the DJ and bouncers.

Speaking of DJs, what the hell was the Hawkman thinking playing Madonna? I gave him a look from across the bar. He nodded and gave me the thumbs up. That was our sign. He faded Madonna and put on my personal anthem: AC/DC's "TNT." It started and I felt my groove.

So Lester was gone. Fuck sakes. I had to feel good about telling the mayor off, and it was one less person on my list of people to ask forgiveness from. I don't know, I was just thinking that now that I had Stephanie, Freda and Snowbird in my life, maybe I could put a few things right.

I don't know why but I was thinking about Sister Regan a lot these days. One day she marched into the room and drew a set of stairs. At the bottom were flames. At the top was the sun and angels. "For everything good you do, like praying or going for confession," she said and tapped the board with her ruler, "you go up one stair. For everything bad you do—like lying (and she looked at me) you go down two stairs closer to hell."

That ended just about every childhood in the room, but for me, that was my sign. Sister Regan was the weak link in the bunch of them, so I made my move to find out the truth through her. I couldn't bear to ask Mom anything. Sister Regan was alone in her office when I cornered her.

"Thou shall not lie," I said. "Who is my father?" Sfen waited outside, guarding the door, and I knew he could hear. We knew who Sfen's dad was. But today was Father's Day and we'd made this trip special to find out.

"Your father," she said. "Didn't your mom tell you?"

"No," I said. "I'm asking you."

"Hazel," she said. "Sit down."

"I'll stand."

"Please."

"I'll stand." I started to shake.

"Let me call Father."

"I want you to tell me. Don't lie."

"Torchy," she took a big breath. "Your mother conceived you from a man who raped her." The tears started to fall. I didn't even feel them coming.

"He had just gotten out of jail. He raped several women in town that week. He used a knife. There was nothing your mother could do."

Sfen and I walked all day. And when we sat down at the rocks and watched the pelicans fly, I was no longer Hazel. Just like how Sfen told me once that the polar bear transformed from the brown bear. Sfen was still Sfen but I transformed into Torchy. His dad just left when Mom told him they were expecting. Just left. Vanished. That was the day we stopped wanting to be priests. That was the day we changed forever.

"Who made you?" I'd ask myself when I looked into the mirror.

"Rape."

"Why?"

"To make me a better weapon."

"Why?"

"To bury the name of Jesus."

That was the fall Sfen and I lit every field on fire where it might have happened. That was the fall when I became Torchy. That was the fall where I said *Fuck you all.*

After I lost Sfen, I think he took something with him. It was more than just his spirit; it was also a lot of my hate and rage. I told Snowbird about it once. That was when he told me about how sometimes you could do more as a spirit than you ever could alive. Maybe my brother came back for the rage I had all the time on his way to the other side. I don't know....

Thelma came back and gave me a huge mug of Coke with ice and a twist of lemon. I smiled and thanked her. "No problem," she said. "You take good care of that girl now."

"I will," I nodded. "Thanks." I ditched the straw and took a huge swallow. It was hard to believe Lester had died after I left. Fuck, he went fast. As much as I wanted to have a shot of liquid tornado, I had to remember that I was broke and it gave me garbage guts, but how could I get some *sombah?* And now, back against the wall, in my old playpen, I could relax, be a man—away from Stephanie and Snowbird.

It had been a while since I had felt a woman's touch, so I took the second story—the secret—that Lester told me nice and slow. Lester had been at the Friendship Festival in Smith this summer. He'd gone there to check out the bands and go on a toot. I knew about the festival. Bands from all over the north and south travelled to Fort Smith for a week to party it up and have a good time. I'd never been to the festival, but I knew if it was in Smith it was going to be a shaker.

To Lester's surprise, Charity was there—away from Vincent, which was a rarity as that fucker never let his woman too far out of his sight for obvious reasons. I guess they'd been scrappin' and she broke loose. Lester ended up sitting with her all day and they even went to the dance together. They had a good time, he said, the best he'd ever had. Charity wouldn't talk about it, he said, but Lester could tell she was lonesome and he crossed his fingers prayin' that this would be his chance.

Because of my meds and a few lucky shots to the head, I don't remember a lot of things in high school, but I do remember that Lester did have his eye on Charity, but, for whatever reason — maybe his seizures, maybe money — she wouldn't go to him. She ran to Vincent, asshole at seventeen. He was a dealer and was making tons of money dabbling in the hard stuff. He could get you anything you wanted — if it was fiscal for him. So he and Charity had been together forever, like a bad habit. I'd never really cared if they made 'er or not but they broke up, got back together, broke up — whatever. All I know is Charity had been on the damage trail ever since.

Anyhow, after Charity and Lester realized that they'd had a little too much to drink to drive back to Simmer, they decided to get rooms at the Pelican, aka Bareback Central. Guess what? With the festival in town there was only one room left with a single bed. So, they agreed to split the bill and Lester offered to take the couch.

As soon as they got in the room, Charity said she needed a shower. Lester turned on the TV but kept the mute button on and prayed to God that she'd come out naked. Well, maybe the Lord above showed some mercy in the face of what was to come for Lester because Charity — and she is very pretty — came out of the bathroom wearing nothin' but a towel.

Let's slow things down a little as it's been so long since I felt the fire of agonizing release. Charity opened the door and walked out with a white towel against her beautiful brown skin and that long brown hair of hers. She wasn't wearing a towel over her head because she wanted the wet look. My God, she walked out and stood defiantly before him. I'm thinking Lester turned the TV off. No — no. He kept it on. He'd be too scared to move. He saw her and she'd put lipstick on to accentuate that pretty face of hers and there they were: her long, smooth legs and lovely painted toes. And she's just standing there, looking at him, eyes locked on him.

She'd decided.

Give me this, Lester was probably thinking. *God, Lord above. Give me this. I'll go to church from now on if you give me this.* Lester said she looked at him with the sweetest eyes and, before he knew it, he whispered, "Drop that towel." And, to Lester's delight, she did.

Lester feasted his eyes on her beautiful breasts, those wicked nipples, each one as hard as a thumb stud on a switchblade, her smooth tummy, her soft everything. To his surprise, Charity had a butterfly tattoo underneath her belly button.

"Wow," Lester said—about her body and the situation, "Nice tattoo."

Charity looked down and ran her hands over her tummy. "Do you like it?" Lester sat up and never felt so Hollywood his whole life.

Charity smiled, blushed and looked back at him. "It's me."

"What?" Lester asked, swallowing hard. "Could you say that again?"

Charity looked at him and he saw a woman filled with secrets and stories and a wish. "Lester," she said, "this butterfly is me." And that's when she walked forward towards him, leaned forward and kissed him.

All of us grew up together just a few grades apart but even in Simmer we somehow become strangers along the way. Boys torture animals, shoot a few ravens, become ninjas for a few summers, get a job, get a car, maybe some road-head, have a kid, shack up, get drunk, get up, fall down, go home.

Girls, though, they grow faster, bloom first. They probably start getting hit on when they're fourteen by the older men in town, figure out how to kiss early. Every girl I ever kissed growing up sure knew how to do it right and sweet long before I ever did. I figure girls start gathering secrets earlier than boys. They've got the power, the *inkwo.* Their bodies bring them attention and they figure out pretty early how the world works. They learn about the hunger of men, how there's no end to it, how possible it is to end up with a pile of wolves on top of you as your terrified eyes glance at the ceiling, the door, the floor. Girls learn their way around men, maybe even before they figure out how to manoeuvre around other women. They figure out things far sooner than the boys and that is the base of their power.

Lester didn't have to tell me. I knew: they made sweet love and all that loneliness Charity had inside her blossomed into giving. She made up for one night with Lester just how lonely she'd been her whole life. She cried after, he said. When he asked her if he should stop, she only held him closer. All night, he said—and he smiled when he told me. *All night*.

I imagine the chalice of her hips receiving him. The heaving and pull, the taking together, the immediate ferocity. I could only imagine how important this was for both of them. After, as the sun rose and the little birds started to sing, calling back the sun, Charity told Lester everything. They had, I guess, a game of truth. She told him about the three brothers who'd tried to rape her one night in Inuvik. She told him about how scared she was that breast cancer ran in her family. Lester listened and couldn't believe she'd welcomed him right inside her. She spoke for a solid two hours about her life and how she just couldn't break free of Vincent. Vincent started beating on her a year after they started going out, and she swore that she'd never live with a man who'd do that. But why couldn't she get away? She didn't even know herself.

"I'm sorry," she said. "I'm doing all the talking. What about you? You know more than anyone what's been on my mind. It's your turn," she said and sat up. "Tell me a secret." Lester said he didn't really have any secrets but he had a confession.

"What's that?" she asked and handed him her smoke.

"I've always loved you," he blushed. "Maybe it's not like that for you, but it's everything to me." And she started crying again. I guess he told her even more. He told her how scared he was for her because he knew how violent Vincent was and how the beatings weren't going to be getting any softer. She showed him her two back molars, the ones on the left in her bottom jaw. They weren't there anymore, and Charity'd never told her family or friends, but Vincent had knocked them out one night when she came home late after visiting her cousin who was passing through town for one night only.

"Promise me," Lester said. "Promise me that you'll leave him. You don't ever have to go with me," he said. "But just promise you'll get away from him."

"I can't," she said. "He needs me."

Then Lester told me something that surprised even him. He pointed to her butterfly tattoo and said, "Butterflies aren't meant for cages." And that's the line that broke her. As the sun met the edges of town, and the morning bloomed into day, she promised him and swore on her mother's grave that she'd leave Vincent and take the time she needed to find herself again. She promised him.

Lester was happy. He said they got up, showered and promised never to tell anyone what happened. They did the deal where the lady leaves the hotel first and you wait half an hour before you go.

"Oh," Charity said before she left the room first. "I owe you half for the hotel bill," she said. "I'll pay you back later."

"Deal," Lester said, and they kissed goodbye. Well, as sweet a story as that was, who was sitting together at the bar just as miserable as ever? Charity and Vincent. I knew they'd be there. I shook my head and thought: what the fuck does Vincent have that Lester wouldn't have given you? Nice fuckin' life, Charity. I hope you can bite back the tears as you grab your ankles and Vince grunts one off, pinning you to your mattress every night.

I thought of the second—and now last—thing Lester had asked of me before he died. I took a big breath and started to get up when, to my surprise, the Inuit who blocked me at the hospital sat down at my table. I was so into thinking about Charity in that towel that I let my guard down. Fucker sat down across from me and nodded. "What are you drinking?"

"What the fuck's it to you?" I growled.

He looked at it and squinted. "Pop?" He motioned to Thelma that he wanted the same thing I had and he ordered me another.

"I'm leaving," I said.

"You can leave in a bit," he said. "We need to talk." The Inuk pulled out his wallet and I took a quick look at his tools: scuffed knuckles, callused hands and black shiny slash scars on his forearms. Looked like he used Plexiglas to try and end it a few times. He was wearing a thick silver ring on each middle finger. He looked strong, stronger than me. And the whole time he was getting his cash out, he didn't take his eyes off me.

Thelma came to us and dropped both drinks off. "He a friend of yours?" she asked me.

"Nope," I said.

"Want me to call Boom?"

"No," I said. "I can handle this."

"You said it." Thelma took the money from the guy and walked away without giving him any change. This didn't faze him a bit. He was breathing through his nose, boring his eyes into me. Trying to intimidate me, I guess. He was thickly built, a heavy hitter for sure. There'd be no strike and stun touch with this guy. He could take anything I had unless I unleashed the sweet science of dirty on him.

"What's your name?" I asked. "Since you obviously know mine."

"Arnie," he said. Neither of us extended our hands. Instead, I calmly took a drink of my pop from my straw, and he did the same.

"To your daughter," he said. I stopped smiling. *How the fuck did he know about Stephanie?*

He watched me. "Easy now. I have a daughter, too."

"Where are you from?" I asked.

"Iqaluit."

I thought of Charity's tattoo. "You guys got butterflies up there?"

"Yeah. We got butterflies. All kinds. We got hornets, caterpillars, bumblebees."

I nodded. "Why are you here?"

"Me?" he took another sip and frowned. "I'm working off my time."

"For what?"

He looked at me. "That's private."

"Uh huh. How much the Bullfrog paying you?"

"Don't matter. I'm not here for the money," he said.

"Oh? Then why are you?"

He looked at me, hard. "I'm here for you." Those daddy-long-leg shivers I felt when we first met came back stronger than ever.

"Uh huh. So this means that sooner or later, you want to down me, right?" He nodded.

"You want the title?" He nodded and actually glowed.

"Look," I said. "I'll be honest. I'm a little busy right now, so how about another time?"

He looked at me and smiled. "Today's the day."

"I'm not going to down you," I said.

"Oh yes you are."

I looked at Charity and Vincent. "I'm busy."

"You have to," he said.

"Why?"

"Because if you don't, the Bullfrog's not gonna tell you where he reburied your brother." He nodded.

A sledgehammer hit my stomach and heart at the same time. I was stunned. "*What?*"

He leaned across the table and growled, "You will fight me today." I looked around the bar, worried someone else might have heard. I've been telling the few who asked that my brother was working in the States and that I was watching his place when really he was buried at the lake.

I tensed. "What the fuck is this?"

"Jeremiah said he was doing some surveying out by the warden's house and he come across a homemade grave." My eyes flashed anger and the Inuit caught that.

"Wolves tried to get at the body, but there were too many rocks." I had an image of wolves with AIDS running through the bush blind and scared.

"Go on," I said. "I know you got more."

"So he dug up the grave to see who it was."

"No..." I said, astonished.

"No head." The Inuit smiled. "Once he saw what was left of your brother's jaw, he buried him again and told a few people."

"Where? Where did he rebury him?"

"The new graveyard."

"In town?" He nodded.

"Who? Who did he tell?"

"Betting men, you could say." I got ready to flip the table up and towards him.

"And told them what exactly?" The Inuk knew the move and placed his arms across the table so I couldn't get leverage.

"Easy now," he said. "All they know is we're gonna fight. And he's going to tell you where he reburied your brother."

I shook my head and cursed my TB. I wanted to fight but was weak. So Sfen's body was in town. Steph and I just walked by there yesterday. "How much did Jeremiah put on this match?"

"Five thousand dollars so far." Good money, but I couldn't win it. Not in the shape I was in.

I nodded. "So where are we supposed to do this?"

"The old racetrack," he said. "Right away—and there's a bonus."

I'll bite. "What?"

"He's spray painted a circle in the sand. It's a big one. If you can take on the whole Smith Squad and me, the pot goes up to ten thousand dollars." Holy fuck. I couldn't believe this.

"Give me a month," I said. "I need to—"

"No deal," Arnie said. "We fight today."

I nodded and began to really think this through. This meant that half the fuckin' town probably knew about the match already.

Whether or not I wanted this, it was going down. I didn't have a choice. I had to keep this asshole talking and process how this was going to work. They had Sfen reburied in the boneyard, but there were a hundred new graves. I saw the tender in the newspaper. My brother was buried. This was good. But where? I remembered that the Bullfrog had the contract to expand the graveyard, so which grave was Sfen in?

My right hand started to feel hot and I realized I was being watched and, fuck me, I was being played right here, right now with the oldest trick in the book. I nodded. "So rather than just meet me out back, why buy me a drink?"

"I've wanted to meet the legend," he said. "I will beat you. I will be the first to knock you out. I thought it was only right I buy you a drink."

"Bullshit," I said. "You bought me a drink to see which hand I throw from, right?"

He smiled and nodded. "You're good."

I nodded. "That's an old trick. As old as the hills, but I got to warn you, I got a hard head. You hit me and the only thing you're going to get is my attention."

He laughed. "You know why I'm going to beat you?"

I sat up. "Tell me."

"You're not hungry anymore." I knew what he was talking about, but I wanted to hear if he could back it up.

I frowned. "I don't get it."

"You got a home now. And that girl. You walk around with that old man. We see you. You look happy. But soft. You're not hungry anymore. Me? I'm starving. We've got Gunner watching your house, by the way. You don't fight, he moves. Maybe he has a nail gun. Maybe there's a house fire and the old blind man can't open any doors cuz they're nailed shut. Think real careful of what your next move is gonna be."

"Fuck you," I said. "And fuck you for even thinking that." *Shit!* Gunner was outside the house. Snowbird's house! With Stephanie and the cat inside. How could they do this to us? I wanted to kill them all but I had to be smart. I had to. Before, I'd run in the lake for a month before a fight and did push-ups on my knuckles to petrify 'em, but what did I have now? I had no strength. No stopping power. All I could do was listen and nod. I used to carry jerry cans filled with water and rocks to strengthen my grip so I could choke slam anyone, but this fuckin' damn TB had fucked me over, I didn't have my summer strength or speed, and it had been too long since I ran The Furnace. I ran my thumbs over both index fingernails. I'd just clipped them. How could I be so stupid and forget my claws? I'd need to use my thumbs if I went for the eyeballs in a ground and pound situation.

"You know—I'm sorry, what was your name again?"

He frowned. He did not like that at all. "Arnie, I said."

"Arnie, I said," I repeated. "No offense but you're boring the shit out of me, but I'll tell you what. Wait right here and I'll be back. If we're going to fight, let me take a piss and I'll return."

"You're going to run," he said. "Your eyes betray you."

"My eyes betray me," I smiled. "That's good. Can I use that later sometime when I'm fucking you over? I won't run, fucker, because you're wrong. How long you been training to down me?"

He answered without hesitation. "A year solid. I started training in lock-up for you."

I smiled. "Well there's my answer."

He stopped smiling. "Your answer to what?"

"I been training my whole life for fuckers like you and this is why you'll lose. I'm hungrier than you'll ever know. To even think you're going to kill a holy man it's already spun back to you. You're already fuckin' dead. You just don't know it yet but half your heart is marked now. Just for talking like that. When you are dying alone and suffering as you rot out shitting pus and dead blood, think of this. Remember this moment. You called black medicine by talking like this." His face whitened and he had a frozen smile on his face. "So you may think you have me, but I have you," I said and knew that got to him. "Now, unless you want to relive the legend of me and my fabulous *piss bomb*, you'll let me urinate in peace until I come back—or do my eyes betray me?"

He didn't like that and let me go. I half walked, half staggered to the bathroom and I did take a piss. Where the hell did that come from? I never spoke like that before. Was the old man with me? How did I know that?

I closed my eyes and felt weak. The earth was spinning. I leaned against the wall and let all my breath out. If I was going to take on the whole Smith Squad—and the Inuk—I'd need an advantage. It had been too long since I'd seen the strange light in the eyes of a man dim as he folds to the earth below him. How could I do this? How would I win? What would Bruce Lee do? My thumbnails were sharp, but I was weak. I'd have to use my Ninjalix of trickery and theatre. I'd have to use their weaknesses against them. I'd look for the signs and line 'em all up before taking my revenge on everyone who had anything to do with today. I did up my fly, and looked at myself in the mirror. Think like a wolf....

I thought of Stephanie and Snowbird. They were only five streets away but there was no way I'd see them until this was done. Ten thousand dollars would settle up all my bills and do something that I should have done a long time ago: bury my brother proper, with ceremony, in the town boneyard with the dignity he deserved.

"Lester," I said to my reflection, "if you're making your rounds, saying goodbye, help me out, buddy. Sfen, someone desecrated your grave. Brother, I need your help. You always told me to think like a wolf. Guide my fists into claws. I don't want anyone to remember you as a suicide and forget about your beautiful, brilliant life.

"Snowbird, if you're listening to the wind," I said, "help."

I then redid my belt but only put the strap back in the three and nine position so when I whipped it out, it wouldn't catch on anything. Think like a wolf....

I then thought of Lester's second request and decided I had to do it now. There was never going to be a good time for this. I walked out

Richard Van Camp

of the bathroom and the Inuk watched me. I made the motion of give-me-a-minute and walked towards Vincent and Charity.

"Hey," I said. Vincent turned, placing himself between Charity and me.

"Hey, Torchy," he said, stiffening up. "How you doin'?"

"Been better," I said.

"How come?" he asked and extended his hand towards the seat across from him. "Have a seat." I sat with Charity between us. Charity made a big show of looking around the bar but she was listening. Vincent was making a big show of trying to act concerned, but he was keeping his eyes and senses on Charity. She probably wasn't allowed to speak or even look at another guy, and she was probably scared she'd get it at home for even sitting across from me. To my surprise, she had a butterfly tattoo on her hand, on the web between her thumb and index finger.

"Nice tattoo," I said.

She immediately put her hand over it and smiled. "Thank you."

"Yeah, I got it for her when we were in Edmonton, hey, hun?" She nodded.

"We're celebrating," he grinned. I'd missed it 'til now: he had snuff at the base of his lip and I saw his black lower teeth when he smiled.

I jumped in. "Nice. You know it's funny," I said. "I heard a friend of mine once say, 'Butterflies aren't meant for cages—'" That got her. She looked at me and her eyes flashed surprise. *How did I know?*

"Huh," Vincent said, sensing something a lot bigger than he was had just blown through his woman. Vincent looked at Charity to see what her reaction was. "Who told you this?" he asked.

"Someone who knew what he wanted," I said. Vincent didn't like that at all. He shifted and, in slow motion, took a drink of his beer and glanced at Charity. Charity looked down.

"Am I missing something?" he asked. "Who are you talking about?" I thought of those two back molars missing from their sockets and how there might be a few more in a few minutes, but there wasn't gonna be an easy way to do this.

"Tell him, Charity." Vincent's head started snapping back and forth between Charity and me, trying to gauge who'd break first. "Go on, Charity—or do you want me to? I won't let him hurt you."

Charity blushed and looked around the room for help. "Who the fuck do you think you are?"

"What the fuck's going on?" Vincent asked. "Charity? Is there something you want to tell me?" Charity looked at me and I didn't blink and I could see something in her that scared me: fear. Absolute fear. But today was the day she was gonna be free.

"Vincent," I said. "See these fingernails of mine?" I used my back to shield them from the Inuk. "I keep my nails nice and long on my index fingers—know why?"

Vincent backed up a bit in his chair. "Let's get back to this—"

"Oh, we'll get there," I said. "I keep my fingernails long so I can disembowel eyeballs if I have to." Vincent's eyes widened. "I can take your eyeball out faster than you can blink. I actually popped a man's eye out once and squeezed it like a hard-boiled egg before handing it back to him." The colour drained out of Vincent's face.

"The reason I'm letting you in on this," I said, "is if I hear that you fuckin' hurt Charity one more time, I will take your eye out—and that's a promise."

"You can't threaten me," he said. "I know where you live."

I smiled. "Tough talk from a small cock," I said. "Now shut up and listen. Charity, you're free. Go home and pack your shit. I made a promise to your silent dove to help you get free."

"Who?" Vincent asked and turned to Charity, this time not hiding his hatred for her. "Who the fuck is he talking about?"

I could tell he wanted to tear into her right there. "Watch it, Vincent. I will fuck you over in a cold hurry."

Charity looked at me with absolute hatred. "Why are you doing this?"

"Do you really want me to speak his name?"

She narrowed her eyes. "I have no idea what you're talking about."

"Really?" I asked. *Fuck,* I thought. *Maybe Lester was wrong.* Maybe he'd lied to get back at me for ruining him. Maybe he made up his little sexcapade with Charity. *Shit! I'd have to smoke her out.*

"Yeah," Vincent said. "We were having a good day until you came up to the table—"

"Lester's dead," I said suddenly, and I said it to her. In a second, time slowed. A mix of emotions washed over her: anger to surprise to shock to grief. In a second I knew that it was all true.

"It seems to me," I said, "you swore on your mother's grave that you'd leave Vincent."

"When the fuck was this?" Vincent growled.

"I have no idea what he's talking about," Charity said and looked at me, but tears started coming down her face. I could tell that she wanted to be anywhere else on this planet except here with us.

"I think you do," I said. "Lester's gone and he wanted you to honour the promise you made him." Vincent's face: he had these white pockets of rage spreading across his cheeks and chin.

He spoke fast and loud, searching her for any cracks in the mask. "Charity, did you fuck Lester? Is that what this is all about—did you?"

"No," she said. "I never—and I never made a promise to leave you. Torchy—fuck off! You're wrecking everything."

Shocked that she'd stay, I said, "Isn't it true that Vincent knocked your back molars out?" Both of their eyes flashed surprise when I said that.

Vincent's jaw actually dropped. "What!" he blurted.

"That was an accident," she said.

The Inuk suddenly stood beside me. "We have to go."

I shot the Inuk the meanest fuckin' look I had. "Give me a minute." He shook his head and looked at the door. Jeremiah and Country stood at the door. "We have to go," the Inuk repeated, this time firmly.

"Back the fuck up," I told him. "You'll get your fight. Just give me one more minute." I had to move fast. The Inuk did back up and sat down, motioning to Jeremiah that we were coming—and I saw his legs. *Ha!* In a second I saw how I'd drop him. It wouldn't be blows to the centre mass or even a nut shot, it'd be his little legs. Typical convict: only worked the pipes and chest when your strength comes from your legs. When I focused my attention back on the table, Vincent was staring into Charity, who was now crying.

"So, Charity, what's it gonna be?" I asked. "Is today the day you break free, or is today the day you finally betray a promise to a man who loved you? And I believe you swore on your mother's grave, right? Doesn't that mean anything to you?"

Vincent started breathing through his nose at this point, and I was no longer a concern to him. I knew that despite my promise to disfigure and blind him that he could not wait to get Charity alone.

"Hun," he said. "Just tell me if he's lyin', baby. Just tell me."

"Yes, Charity," I echoed. "Just tell him if I'm lying." Charity was cornered and she was now sweating as well as crying. I thought of that butterfly below her belly button and I thought of her in that towel as she stood before Lester in the Fort Smith hotel room. Her hair spilling across her brown shoulders must have been something.

She shook her head and looked defiantly at Vincent and me. "Torchy's lying, Vince. I never fucked around on you. Torchy's a liar."

"Is that my kid you're carrying?" Vincent asked. "Is it?" Charity covered her face and burst into tears. My eyes bugged. *"What?"*

Vince looked at me. "We were celebrating." He fished around in his pocket and pulled out a piece of paper. He slammed it down on the table, face up. It was an ultrasound of a little soul. "We just came from the hospital and got a fuckin' picture of my baby in her tummy." He then swung his head to Charity and peeled his lips back into a scowl. "Whose fuckin' kid is inside of you?"

Oh fuck! I shook my head and thought of Lester. I looked at Charity's drink: it was ginger ale, not beer. I couldn't back down now or I'd lose for sure, and I made a promise to Lester. "If there's a credit card receipt at the hotel in Smith with Lester's name on it from this summer during the Friendship Festival—and you were there, weren't you, Charity? Where did you sleep that night?" Charity's jaw dropped, and Vincent stared at her completely still.

I continued. "Lester's gone, Charity, and he loved you." I reached into my pocket and took out Lester's gold chain and cross. Charity looked at it and said nothing. "You know Lester was a Mountain Dene. When one of them dies, their loved ones get to keep one thing of theirs." Charity looked at that chain and started crying again. "Lester loved you somethin' fierce, and he asked me to give this to you. He also asked that you help out his mother when she's ready to burn the rest of his things."

She started crying again, and that was all that Vincent needed. "Fuck sakes, Charity," he said. "For fuck sakes—you did fuck around on me. You fucked Lester, didn't you?"

"Shut up, Vincent," I said. I handed the gold chain and cross to Charity and she took it. She started shaking. It was like she couldn't hear Vincent. She took it and looked at it and then looked at me. Tears started spilling out of her eyes.

"He wanted you to have this, Charity. That was the last thing he asked me to do, not even an hour ago. You were his last wish." She started crying again, and I walked away. I looked at the Inuk and pointed towards the door. He nodded and started to make his way there. I glanced at his legs again and decided that this was how I was gonna dish out some fuck-you-tender.

"Fuck you, Torchy," Vincent spat.

I looked at Vincent. "I'm keeping my promise."

He looked at me, arms crossed and shaking. "Which fuckin' one?"

"If I hear that you hurt Charity, I will blind you." I looked at Charity. She was speechless. She held onto that chained cross and said nothing.

I spoke quick. "My promise is only good for a week. After that, it's out of my hands." I looked at Charity. "If you're gonna stay, you're on your own."

Vincent started feeling tough and he tried to stand, but I whipped around and sliced his cheek with my thumb. He yelped and grabbed his face, sitting down. "Could have been your eye, fucker," I growled and stood before walking towards the door.

I turned and looked at Charity. "One week, starting now. If you're gonna make a break for it, you're under my protection. If not…" I held my arms out and shrugged. "Think of your baby. Remember what Lester told you: butterflies aren't meant for cages." She looked at me and started to shake her pretty little head while Vincent got up to go to the bathroom. His blood was seepin', and it was out of my hands now, completely in hers.

The Inuk was smiling as I made my way into the Suburban. "Nice work," he said. "I didn't know you could move so fast."

"Fuck you," I growled and let my snake eyes shine. "You want to inherit the beast?" He stepped back. "Let's go so I can give it to you." He tried to shrug my words off but it was too late. My words hit him and I felt a lot of his confidence leave.

I walked in front of him and gritted my teeth. "I had no fuckin' idea Charity was pregnant, Lester. You're gonna be a dad, buddy. Even in heaven, you're gonna be a dad."

I took the front seat of the Suburban I had seen Jeremiah use to patrol the streets of Simmer my whole life. He drove with his two canes across the dashboard. I took the front and the Inuk and Country sat behind me.

"No hard feelings, eh?" Jeremiah asked as we sat in the Suburban. There was a walkie-talkie on the dash, probably for Gunner standing outside the house.

"Fuck you," I said. "Where's my brother?"

"Take it easy," he said and smiled. "I told you: he's been reburied in the new graveyard."

"Where?" I asked.

"Now now," he said. "I'll tell you after the fight."

I looked at him. "I could go to the cops. Tell them you're tampering with the deceased."

"He's got a permit to move bodies," Country said.

Jeremiah smiled. "You could go to the cops, but I'd never tell you where he was. You know, my first wife was Dogrib. Before she died—God rest her soul—she taught me a lot about their ways. Hell, I'm probably more Dogrib than you are with all I know." He and Country started snickering. The Inuk was murderously quiet. Fuck, I didn't like having my back to either one of them.

I glanced at Jeremiah's black coffin shoes. For as long as I could remember, the Bullfrog had bad feet. He'd come to the pool sometimes for the hot tub, and it was always closing time for me and Sfen when he'd sit up and you could see his feet: gaiter toes, all branched out like broken twigs. That was another reason he got his nickname: he has to wear customized coffin shoes that look like they were made for elephants. They're boxes more than shoes, padded with foam and supports. They remind me of the shoes Frankenstein wore, and I give thanks to the spirits for cursing such an evil man with bad feet. That's what you get, fucker, for making a life of continuously fucking good people over.

"Don't you worry, Torchy," Jeremiah said. "Before the day is out, you'll know where your brother is buried. I knew to bury him with his feet closest to the cross. Dogribs believe this way your spirit can pull itself up, use those arms on the cross like a ladder and pull yourself up to the sky."

I looked at him. He was being serious. "I wouldn't desecrate a grave, Torchy," he said solemnly. "I buried your brother right. Fight this fight today and we'll call it even. And you may even make some cash." He looked at me and grinned.

I shook my head. "I'll fight all right," I said. "But you're going to regret ever touching my brother's body."

He chuckled and shook his head. "And you're going to regret making a fool out of me and the mayor. And Arnie here is gonna put the dog bite on you."

At that, Arnie the Inuk started barking like a dog into my ear. "Arr Arr Arrrr!" Nothing out of the Pollywog. Once again, he wasn't too thrilled about being second place.

I just stared ahead and shook my head. "Fuck, you're dumb," I said to them all.

The Pollywog was an interesting case. Country was in training to fight at the UFC. His dad was always flying him out for various training camps. Judging from the cauliflower ears that were swollen and purple, and seeing at least twenty pounds of new muscle, they must have been honing him to be a modern-day gladiator. Country used to scrap all the time growing up and he was a beast. He and his heavy hands have never been put down. And that's his claim to fame. I know he wanted to down me. Word was out two summers ago he was gonna try, but he never came for me. Lord knows, I trained even harder just in case. But ever since he started his training, he quit fighting in town and that said a lot. That said he was turning pro and he wouldn't waste a split knuckle on a local boy's tooth and risk infection or a criminal record. They say he got his hands registered as lethal weapons, but that had to be gossip. Still, I had to be wary of him. He kicked the Horflet boy so hard his heart moved to the other side of his chest. And that was a few years ago outside the Terminal.

We made our way out to the back road that would lead us to the old racetrack. The men were quiet and I shook my head. I took a big breath and let it out. I needed to think. My head was under attack still from what happened at the bar. So Charity was pregnant. Wouldn't that be something if that baby was Lester's and that was what set her free? It was her choice now. I'd given her a window to get away.

I closed my eyes and took another deep breath. I had to watch their range, I thought. Dangerous hands. Dangerous reach. I had to watch it, but all I really wanted to do was sleep. I did the thing where I clear my head and start a new feeling, and the feeling I chose was quiet.

It was August. Sfen was now buried in town. Moose and caribou antlers would be in velvet. You listen to the old man and you learn new things every day: next month was the moon when the geese flew. This is the moon when wolf pups that are too small get left behind by their packs. The bigger ones leave with the adults to learn how to hunt and track. The ones who were too little would be left behind to die. We dropped tobacco for them just two days ago. And this was the moon when the bison did the same. Mothers and calves began the long haul towards the winter ranges. Their lives are braided—

"You know, Torchy," Jeremiah said, "Lester's in a better place."

"Fuck off," I said.

"It's a shame Lester fought so hard. The boy suffered…" I shook my head.

"I suppose you got your information on the subdivision from him, hey?"

"None of your business."

"Well, he's wrong. We moved those rocks."

"Then you'll die too," I said. "Eaten alive by cancer. Good."

Country made a move to punch me, but Jeremiah raised his hand. "Hey, Torchy," Jeremiah said. "There's no need to talk like that. Now I found your brother's body and I put it in the graveyard for you."

"Fuck you!" I said. "You should have left him."

"For what—the wolves? They'd been trying to get him," he said. "And I couldn't let that happen. What did you do? You left him out there alone in an unmarked grave. Why? Ashamed he killed himself? Or did you blow his head off for him?"

Before I could hit him, Country got me in a full nelson and started squeezing the air out of my head. I couldn't breathe and stars started popping around my eyes. They bugged and my arms started to tingle.

"Now look," Jeremiah said. "I'll tell you where I buried him once you do this. Win or lose. I'm not such a bad guy." He patted his breast pocket. "I've drawn out a map of the graveyard and I've marked out where we put him."

I was getting ready to pass out when Jeremiah said, "Let him go, son. He'll need all his strength to take you on."

Country let me go and slammed my head into the dashboard. The stars were swirling and I leaned hard against the window. I blinked away the protozoas of light I saw in front of me and felt the TB enzymes take hold of my weakness.

Jeremiah smiled. "You're probably wondering where the Big Dance is happening, hey? Well, it's at the old racetrack," he said. "We got her nice and pretty for you."

I rolled my eyes and took a big breath, filling my lungs with shitty air. *The Big Dance?* I could feel the Inuk watching me. If I could keep getting his adrenaline to dump, I could get it to backfire, tucker him out before we got there. Jeremiah glanced in the rear-view and spoke: "The rules are genius really. You take on my boy Arnie here, you get five grand. You take on him and the squad, you get ten grand. Either way, I'll tell you where I buried your brother."

I dry swallowed and rubbed my head. "Any rules I should be aware of?"

He shrugged. "Once you're out of the circle we've painted on the ground, you're out. If you beat my boys and leave, I don't owe you a penny. It's gotta be every man out before you collect."

I glared at the Inuk. "So that means this is all or nothing. I thought I'd get five grand by beating the Squad and then five for beating the champ here."

Jeremiah shrugged. "Rules changed, I guess. All or nothing. No stand-stills, either."

I was quiet. It was going to either get really bloody or really dirty, and I didn't want to bleed today. Bloody fights were the worst cuz you could be downing them forever with lupus in the blood or Hep. I nodded. "Anything else?"

"Boss," the Inuk said. "No belts." I sat up. *Shit—*

"Torchy's rigged his so he can whip it out fast and none of the boys wear any."

The Bullfrog looked in the rear-view and smiled. "No belts, Torchy." I looked at the Inuk and he flexed his muscles.

"That's okay, fucker," I said and undid the button on top of my fly. "You got your weapons. I got mine." Shit, I thought. I was weak, tired, and pissed off. I didn't have a chance in Hell. *What would a sick wolf do?*

As we took the small road to the old racetrack, I saw trucks and cars parked alongside the road. There must have been thirty vehicles at least. People were walking towards the racetrack or climbing Panty Point, a rise above the racetrack you could look down from. There in the ditch were little old ladies and their grandkids with empty ice cream buckets picking berries.

Then I heard the music blaring. As we got closer, I rolled down the window to hear it. Jeremiah and his son started to giggle when it became clear. It was the Rocky soundtrack blaring away. "Na na na! Na na naaa."

"Christ," I thought and looked at Jeremiah. "Are you selling tickets for this?"

He smiled and shook his head. "It's free, but if you want to bet you can."

"You're gonna lose today," Country said. "Ten thousand dollars says so."

"The dog bite's comin'," Arnie whispered.

"Take it fuckin' easy," I said. Jeremiah got his Suburban as close to Panty Point as he could and then he had to park. I got out and stood in the sun.

Immediately, townies walked by me and nodded. "Good luck, Torchy."

"Good luck."

"Man up. You can do 'er!"

"Give 'er!" I looked away. I watched the little old ladies in the ditches picking berries with their grandkids. I thought maybe when this was over we could do the same with Steph.

And then along came Andy, the fire chief, and his wife. Time was catching up on Andy but he was still dyeing his hair black. "Howdy, Torchy," he said and shook my hand.

"Howdy," I said.

"This is Terese," he said. "My wife."

Terese stood with a beer in her hand and a lit smoke in the other. "Hi."

When we were kids, Andy used to come over after midnight and pick Sfen up and cruise for hours. Andy hired Sfen to paint a flame job on his truck and he did. It took a few weeks and it was gorgeous to see the flames grow and grow. The flames licked all the way up to the windshield on the front hood and sides. Andy had an airbrush system in his shop at the college, and Sfen started coming home later and later. This was when Andy was married to June. I'd wait up for Sfen for as long as I could, but I'd always fall asleep on the couch.

I caught them once and that was when I was raking leaves. I come around the back of the house and they were locked up with their tongues hollowing each other's mouths out. Their eyes were closed and Andy's hands were down the front of Sfen's pants. "Whoah," I said out loud and they stopped. Andy pulled his hands out of Sfen's pants so fast and pushed my brother away. I dropped the rake and walked back into the house.

Sfen and I never talked about it but three days later I come home to find Sfen crying in the tub with a straight razor on the ledge. Fuck, I beat Sfen bad. That was the second time I caught him trying to kill himself and I let him have it good. There he was, naked, crying in the bathroom and I started slapping him across the head.

"What the fuck?" I asked when I seen what he was gonna do. I flew towards Sfen and pulled him out of the water. "You gonna leave me all alone, huh, Sfen? After all we been through?"

"Stop it," he said, not even defending himself. "Leave me alone."

"You're my big brother, goddamnit. You're gonna end it over Andy?"

"'He doesn't love me,'" he sobbed.

I cuffed him hard. "So what? He's fuckin' married, you gaylord."

Sfen covered his head. "Why? Why doesn't he want me anymore?"

I yelled, "Cuz I caught you homo'ing out, that's why. He's worried I'm gonna tell and his ol' lady's gonna find out!"

Sfen looked at me. "What am I gonna do, Torchy?" he asked and started crying so helplessly. I looked at him with disgust. My big brother crying, naked.

I handed him a towel. "Don't kill yourself over Andy. You'll find someone, Sfen. I promise you will." Sfen covered his face and sobbed. I wrapped the towel around him.

When he wouldn't stop crying, I hung my head. "Fuck sakes, Sfen. For fuck sakes. Don't you ever kill yourself."

"I'm sorry," he said.

"You're all I have," I said. And then he started crying some more.

"Come on," I said. "Aren't we going to Hawaii?" Sfen pressed his palms into his eyes.

"Come on," I said. "You promised. And what does the Bible say about that, huh? You're always reading the Bible. What does it say?" He shook his head.

"And, fuck sakes, you promised since you were ten that we'd go to Hawaii and swim with the dolphins and those fuckin' turtles. Fuck, you're the one who told me those manta rays got the faces of bears. We were supposed to have them fly over us underwater and look up together, 'member?" My voice choked and I got tears. He nodded.

"That's right. You promised we'd go there and get tattoos, too."

He nodded and smiled. "I promised."

I led my brother to his room, helped him lie down, sat with him all afternoon and talked to him. That night I cooked up some soup and toast and rented *Heat*, cheered him up, and Andy never showed his face around our house again. But every once in a while, when he was drinking, he'd call the house for Sfen. I'm sure he got through when I wasn't around, but I'd hang up when he'd ask, "Is your brother home?"

I looked at Andy and his wife and he could tell what I was thinking. He swallowed hard, afraid I'd tell on him. "Good day for a rumble," he said. I looked ahead and nodded, worried my eyes would show my concern. "They been clearing this racetrack for days," he said.

I nodded. "How'd you hear about it?"

He looked at his wife. "Word's been out for days," he said. "We got family come in from Hay River. Why don't you see if they're here, hun?"

Terese looked at him and smiled. She looked at me and took a sip of her beer. "We bet on you," she said and put her hand on my shoulder. "Good luck." I nodded. She walked up the hill.

"They say there's an old bear around here," Andy said and pointed west. "He lives here all alone."

"No mate?" I asked.

"No mate," he said. "Maybe he'll give you strength."

I looked at the bush. "Maybe." That bear'd be on the clock: looking for a den, trying to get fat. I thought of Snowbird. "Can I bum two smokes?" I asked.

"Sure," he patted his breast pocket and pulled two out. "How's your brother? Is he still in the city?" I looked at Andy and I saw a lonesome man. Even with Terese he was still lonely.

"Yeah," I said. "He's got a good job. He's in love."

Andy was shocked. "Really?"

"Yup," I said. And that was like a bullet to him. I saw all of him in a second: hunger, disappointment. Andy hung his head and swallowed hard.

"I gotta go," I said and made my way up the hill. Think like a wolf....

Gunner was standing outside Snowbird's. I had to do this. I thought of that old bear and decided to pray to him. He was probably watching, sleepy but starving.

"*Sah*," I said in Dogrib. "I got Super Grover arms and I cannot even connect with authority like I used to. Please give me an edge. Please. I'm open to attack on all sides. These are mean men and they're making me fight for my family and for money. Just give me an edge. Anything. Now is a time for tombstone courage. Please help me. I honour you with this pitiful offering in all of your grace. Help me and my family." And I laid the two cigarettes at the base of some yarrow to bless the earth before us. The fighting ground. The proving ground. The earth Sfen and I crossed to go hunting ptarmigan in the winter.

I touched the earth for Sfen.

I touched the earth for my mom.

I touched the earth for Lester.

I touched the earth for Snowbird and Stephanie. I stood up, took a big breath. This was going to be a hyena war.

Ever since they started handing out mikes to the human gorillas on WWF and WWE, everyone had to make a speech up north before going toe to toe. Outside the bars, out at the bush parties, out at the landslide, everybody had to make a speech. Right now, the Bullfrog was making a speech to pretty near half the town with a whole pile of guests from Hay River and Smith. There were even trucks pulled up that had Alberta licence plates.

This must have taken some time. Someone had mowed the grass in the middle of the racetrack while somebody had spray-painted a circle in fluorescent orange that was actually pretty small. I thought it would be bigger so I couldn't keep running, but it was actually a good fightin' one. It would be close quarters. That used to be my advantage: dirty boxing.

Jeremiah had rigged up a wireless mike to two huge speakers he had on the tail of his truck. They hummed and popped when he spoke and they were loud. I spotted the walkie-talkie hanging off his hip, the one that linked him to Gunner who was standing outside Snowbird's.

"All right, folks! Welcome to the Big Dance!" He smiled. "We got a local legend here today. Fort Simmer's very own, Torchy." There was applause. A lot of folks stood outside the circle while some folks brought lawn chairs. A small breeze kept the bugs away and the sun was high in the trees.

"I'm sure you know that Torchy has a record of twenty-two knock outs. This man has never been defeated. Not yet. The same goes for my son, my boy!" The crowd cheered. "Fort Simmer's very own and UFC hopeful: Country!" The Smith Squad didn't look too confident with the news that Country was going to fight, as well, and this could be used to my advantage. Twenty-two knock outs? Wow. The truth was I'd only knocked out eight men, but that was Simmer for you: a gossipy garden ripe with hyperbole. To my shame, Lester was my first K.O., and I had no idea how I was going to knock anyone out today.

Jeremiah bellowed, "The last man standing in this circle gets ten grand! So it's every man for himself."

Four members of the Smith Squad were walking around with bags and boxes, writing down bets and chatting with the crowd. The Inuk, who was by far the most dangerous, stood in the centre of the circle, glaring at me. I should have said "No rings" as a rule, but it was too late.

Country pointed at me and made the motion of snapping something huge in half. *Shit.* He was a little slow in the eyes but don't you believe it, not for a heartbeat. Those eyes were a gateway to something cruel and calculating. He loved to issue misery with those fists and his eyes had the same look of fascination you see in boys torturing ants with fire or pulling the wings off of flies. He loved to break men down and right now he was grinning, smiling at me.

The others were just a ragtag of what-could-have-beens. They'd be easy. No problem. In fact they were all torqued up—chain-smoking, too—and that would catch up with them fast when we squared off. Time was my ally here because the longer we waited, the heavier their bodies would feel when we got to it. Their legs would feel like lead and their arms would feel like they were underwater, and I'd do the fuckin' water dance on their heads because I was the master of my adrenaline. My meds helped with that. I had impulse control like never before because of my meds, and the thing I noticed was the Inuk never warned them about my nails. He wasn't a team player and was looking out for himself. He wanted that ten grand and wasn't about to share.

"Okay," the Bullfrog said. "Once again, thank you all for coming to the Big Dance!" The crowd cheered. "My boys are taking bets and the pot is the same. I repeat: the last man standing in this ring gets ten grand. Once they step outside of the circle, they're out."

The Inuk stood tall and was doing light stretches. Country stood beside him. The other men were finishing up taking bets and marking them all down on little notepads. And there was the box from the Northern. An egg box of all things, holding ten grand.

I looked up and there was a jet flying overhead. When I saw one I always wondered where they went. Someone in first class was ordering another round. Families were heading on vacation. I remember Sfen and I used to lie on the snow and wonder out loud where they were all heading. "Anywhere but here," he'd say. "Maybe Hawaii."

"When are we going again?"

"When I get the money," he said. "I promise." I'd always shake my head but secretly wish it could come true —

"Torchy," Jeremiah said. "How 'bout that belt?" I looked at him. Shit, I tranced out. I looked around before whipping my belt out slowly and the crowd "oohh'd" because they saw that I had planned it as a weapon. I looked around and started towards Country and he backed up. The rest of the boys all looked at Jeremiah and he nodded. "Bets are over. Everybody get in that circle." They did but not before handing him the egg box and the notepads.

"Come on, Torchy," Jeremiah said. "Play fair."

"What about the Inuk's rings?" I called. "He's gonna lose those, or what?"

The Bullfrog shook his head and I saw his fat quiver around his chin. "Nope. He's a married man and that wouldn't be Christian of me, now would it?" He held out his hand and covered the mike. "Come on, son. Ten grand and his rings stay. Now hand that belt over."

"Up yours," I said and shook my head. I was surrounded. I handed him the belt and my pants started to loosen. Being Dogrib, I didn't have an ass at all. I was straight nuts and ribs. Without my belt and with my TB, my pants started to slide. Suddenly, I was surrounded by a warm wind. I thought of Stephanie and our monkey dance and I got me an idea. My pants fell to my knees and everyone started to laugh. I made a big show of being embarrassed and tried pulling them up. The Smith Squad was laughing. Jeremiah was laughing—even Country. Everyone laughed except the Inuk. I pulled them up but they fell down again. I looked around and acted all frustrated and this got the whole crowd laughing. The orangutan in me started to feel a little frisky.

"Boss," the Inuk said. "It's a trick. He's gonna do the piss bomb." Jeremiah and his crew stopped laughing.

"That's right," the Inuk said. "It's a trap."

"No trap," I said and looked around. "No piss bomb. I got TB. I lost too much weight and that's why I need my belt."

"Nope," Jeremiah said. "No belt for you. Now let's get it on."

"Wait," I said as I struggled to pull my pants up. "I want to say something."

"Too late," the Bullfrog said.

"Oh come on, Jeremiah!" Stan the Man called out. "He's got his pants around his ankles for God's sakes."

"Yeah," someone else called out. "Let him speak."

Before I knew it, people started to chant: "Speech! Speech! Speech!" Jesus Christ—for once this town was getting along.

Jeremiah looked at me and shook his head. "Okay okay," he said and handed the mike to me. "Shit sakes," he said all red-faced under his breath. I took the cordless with my right hand while my left held up my pants. Everybody in the audience leaned forward to listen.

"As you know, I have been very sick these past few months. I got TB." The crowd murmured amongst themselves. I could see the Smith Squad warming up. Some were stretching. One of them was jumping up and down. Country was wrenching on his nipples and wincing, just twisting on them to get himself all jacked up.

"It's okay," I said. "Thank you for your concern. I'm on the horse pills and I'm slowly recovering." People nodded and a few started to clap. "There are two side effects to these pills. First, I lost weight. A lot, so I'm not in the best shape."

"You'll get there, Torch!" someone called.

"Thank you," I said and dropped my pants to my ankles. "But I wanted to tell you all that I have a love now. I have a family. And the mistake Jeremiah and his crew made was they put all of you and this between me and my home." I stepped out of my shoes and stepped out of my pants before putting my shoes back on. I was now standing in front of a crowd of at least fifty townies in my gonch, shoes and Sfen's shirt. "Because even a dying man will fight with his last breath to get home. To feel the love of his family." I could feel the wind pick up as the crowd fell silent. All eyes turned to Jeremiah. *Look at me,* I thought: I was suddenly the Karaoke King of Fort Simmer. Give me a mike and I was practically Elvis. "The other side effect of these pills," I said, "is they give you sweaty balls." The crowd hushed. Somebody whistled. I dropped the mike and, with my right hand, reached in and started to scratch my bad boys, making a big show of it. The crowd hissed and "awww'd."

"What the?" Jeremiah asked. I then held the offending append-age—my fingers—up for everyone to see as I dropped my gonchies to my thighs.

"Holy fuck!" Country said.

"Just like Jesus said." I looked around. "Let the clean be clean, and let the filthy be filthy." I charged all the men in the ring, fuckin' homophobes. I did the monkey dance and wiggled my head back and forth with my arms out and I waddled towards them. I even made the "Oo Oo Oo!" sounds and started air humping as I waddled. I bruised my scrotum as I dry humped the memory of where they'd all been standing. And they started running. I chased those boys good and, before we made 'er one loop, the Smith Squad all scrambled out of the circle for the Suburban. They were out before they knew it was over—including Country, and before Jeremiah could warn them, it was done.

Well, almost…. I only had the Inuk to worry about. He hadn't moved an inch.

"Fuck sakes!" Jeremiah started hopping up and down. "Fuck sakes anyways, you fuckin' dumb assholes! She was a trick. Now you're disqualified!"

I smiled and looked around. The crowd "ooooh'd" again and everyone started to clap. People started whistling. They'd just seen a Dogrib miracle—namely my peenee. It was ridick and majestic all at the same time. They knew that half the show was over, and the real show was about ready to begin—and it had just escalated in less than a minute. I looked at the Inuk and he was centered. I could feel it. How this fucker knew not to move was beyond me. I had to stay out of his reach. Five grand, mama. Now I was aimin' for ten.

"Sorry, boss!" the men said. "Sorry, he fuckin' tricked us!" I pulled my gonch back on as fast as I could.

"Yeah—" one of them started to say, but then we heard the screaming. We all looked. Even the Inuk. It was screaming all right, and it was coming from Country. He'd planted his feet wide and had his fists by his sides. He screamed with the fury of someone who should have known better. He screamed from the belly of a giant who'd been outsmarted and defeated. He looked like King fuckin' Kong. All that was missing was the chest beating.

Oh. I take that back. He started beating his chest and hollering, "Fuck you, Torchy!"

"He's never been put down," Jeremiah yelled. "You all saw. That was a technical win, but he didn't put my boy down!" I took the moment to look at Arnie, the last man in the circle, the last man in the way of ten grand. And he stood there calmly, biding his time, thinking of the fastest way to throw me over that line — *if* he didn't want to punish me first.

He really wanted to hurt me, and, underneath this all, he had my respect. I wouldn't give it any more room than that, but I had to stay away from that reach of his. I couldn't use my standard-issue chin music, but I had to get him out of that circle.

He nodded at me. "Smart." I closed my eyes and nodded my head twice, letting the cocaine gland spill. I snapped my sockets open: *Snake eyes*. I stood there, ready to chuck some knuckles in a way they'd never suspect.

"Get him!" Jeremiah said. "Get him! That fucker just cost me five grand." That would take care of my bills, but I wanted that full ten K to take care of my brother's body. I had to stay and those fuckers knew it. The Inuk smiled with this knowledge and started to come at me. He used his thumbs to turn those silver rings over and they revealed a single polar bear claw as big as my ear on each ring.

Fuck! I'd been so busy staring at his legs that I missed his hands. "No fair," I said. "Those are illegal."

"Not where I come from," he grinned. I moved away and we started to circle each other. I had one move. The worst move ever. It'd take all I had and I did not want to do it. I flicked my thumbs out and knew the daggers of them were strong. To my surprise, he did the same. He had claws either way, be it swipe or punch, backhand or bare-knuckle. This cocksucker could flat-line me if I wasn't careful. He changed his breathing. Only now did he breathe through his mouth. This was so he wouldn't overheat or power-out, and we circled each other.

"You don't have to do this," I said. "You can still walk away. Don't make me do what I can." He grinned.

"I'm warning you," I said. "You'll never be the same. Think of your daughter."

He smiled. "That's why I'm fighting. To be a legend, you gotta beat a legend." *Shit!*

Jeremiah started to yell. "Get him! Don't just dance around. Get him!" The Inuk glared to his left. He didn't enjoy getting yelled at like a dog. I saw this and felt some hope. I had one shot.

"Come on," I egged him. "Come and get me!"

Country saw this and built on it. "Yeah! Get him! Get that fucker!"

I called out to Arnie, "Split it with me. Split the pot. I'll give you five grand. Think about it. Just walk out of that circle and you'll be set. No lies." The Inuk thought about it.

"Keep moving!" Jeremiah yelled. "Hurt him!"

"Come on," I said and put a lock dot with my mind on his right thigh. "You could send that money home. Think of your daughter. This could be sweet for both of us. If you don't win, you don't get any money and I'm gonna fuck you up. You get nothing either way. Don't make me do this. We're talking complete disfigury."

"You're wrong," he grinned. "I'll have beaten you."

"Fine," I said and spit on both of my fists. "My TB's still active and I'm gonna give it to you."

"Already had it," he grinned. "I'm immune." Fuck! Who was this guy—Terminator 8, I guess! He started advancing.

"Get him, you fuckin' cuggy!" Jeremiah yelled. "Are you gonna stand around and fuck a dead seal or are you gonna fuck him up?"

Everything stopped. Even time. The Inuk froze and somebody hissed. "Cuggy" was the worst thing you could ever call an Inuk and the crowd stood silent. Jeremiah stopped. The Inuk stopped and that was his mistake. I focused, inhaled and spun, and caught him with a knee stun: a swift, incapacitating blow with my sharp Dogrib knee into Arnie's inside thigh. I heard a pop. With flying hands, I shot the heel of my hand into the bridge of his nose. Blood flew. It wasn't pretty and I wasn't proud of it, but when his body lifted, I seen the afternoon sun on the earth where he'd been standing before he slumped to the ground, I stomped those polar bear claw rings of his until they broke, and then I went to town on his hands, stomping on them over and over. Arnie never made a sound.

I gave it everything I had. My snake eyes burned to infinity as I dished out vengeance. I let the bad man in. I went Bazook. It felt, after a while, like I was stomping wet rubber until somebody cried, "Leave 'im alone, Torchy! Jeezus, he's had enough!"

That broke the trance.

I cleared my head. The Inuk was out cold, and there was blood everywhere: he looked like a dead bear with his tongue like that. I didn't feel anything physically, just a faraway throbbing in my right hand. I had somehow busted it on his big walrus head.

The racetrack was quiet. Nobody said nothing. There was half a tooth in the sand and it sure wasn't mine. The townies had just witnessed a small town boot fuck and that was always a shocker no matter how many times you saw it.

I walked up to my jeans and picked them up. My right hand clicked and I paused. I'd torn some ligs. I had to use my left hand to get the jeans under my arm. I also walked up to Jeremiah and took my belt from him. How I wish I had a camera as both he and the entire Smith Squad had their mouths dropped open.

"Which grave did you bury my brother in?" I asked. Jeremiah was frozen.

"Hey, fucker," I repeated. "Which grave is Sfen in?"

He looked at me with disgust. "The one to the left of your mother's."

I nodded. "Tell Gunner I did all you asked. Tell him to leave my family alone." He nodded, his eyes buggin'.

"Do it." I motioned with my chin towards his walkie-talkie.

He pulled it out and spoke into it, watching the blood drip onto my shoes. "Gunner, this is me. Leave the girl and the old man alone. It's done."

"Roger," Gunner said. "Over and out, boss. Did they whoop him?"

"Just fuckin' do as you're told," he said.

"Ten-four."

Had I not been so suddenly tired from the adrenaline dump, I would have done something about this to all of them. I turned and motioned for Jam Can, the old road dog and brains behind Lucky 7 Cabs, to grab my clothes and put them in the box with the ten grand. "Good job," he nodded.

He handed the box of cash and my clothes to me. "Time is it?"

He looked at his watch and we both saw that his hand was shaking. "Five thirty."

I could still make supper. My head felt light and I started to sway. "Figure I can get a ride to the store?"

"Sure," he nodded. "Don't bleed on my seats."

"Well let's fuckin' go then." Someone started their truck, breaking the silence. Then everyone did.

I walked with Jam Can to his cab and I could smell my own sweat: high and dark. Rust. The blood on my legs was getting sticky. I started to smell wet pennies. It was a good fight, mean but necessary. Trucks started to pull away from the racetrack and I only glanced back once.

The Smith Squad started to lay the boots to the Inuk. I don't know if he was swimming back to consciousness or if he was still out, but they were giving it to him pretty good. Well, I'd warned him....

"That was a good one," Jam Can smiled in the rear-view mirror. "A classic." I looked at my hand. It was busted all right, swelling fast and good. I couldn't move my middle finger and my thumb was straight out.

"Where to?" I knew the waiting room'd take forever, and my meds were at Sfen's trailer. If I could get those and pop two, I could wait forever until I got plastered up. "Trailer court," I said.

"Need any booze? Cigs? I could get them for you." I could see his eyes in the rear-view focused on my cash. "Drop me off at my brother's trailer," I said.

"I can wait. You better go to the hospital."

"I can walk." I didn't want any lechery. I was rich, finally. I could get what needed doin' done. In style, too. My body hummed. I was all out of steam. I needed my meds....

Sfen's trailer smelled a little stale. I opened the side window and went to the back bedroom. Oh, my hand throbbed. I didn't even try to flex. There on the nightstand were my meds. I popped two and dry swallowed. I then went to Sfen's closet and carefully grabbed his workout bag. I sniffed it and there he was: cologne, sweat, salt. His scent in the leather. I used my left hand to scoop all the cash into it. Ten grand and then some. Today was my day: Sfen would be given a proper burial and I had the money to do it right. I looked at Sfen's nightstand and there was his Bible. I grabbed it and tossed it in the bag. If I was going to the hospital, I'd be there for hours. Maybe I could read with my good hand. I was so suddenly tired and I couldn't open or close my fist. I slowly pulled on Sfen's favourite shirt and my track pants. This took forever with one hand. I then headed to the washroom for a drink and some peroxide. My main knuckle was busted, too swollen to bleed, but the fucker was deep cut and I had to disinfect myself. I knew I should be using ice, but I figured the doc would give me something better. Fuck, my hand looked rough. It was swole and shiny.

I grabbed the bag and was about to walk out the door when I saw Country walk into Sfen's living room with a Molotov cocktail in his right hand and a claw hammer in his left. He didn't know I was home. Before I could say anything, Country threw the cocktail at Sfen's TV and it exploded on impact, spraying fire on the curtains and carpet. Country jumped back, surprised with the radius of the splash.

"What the fuck!" I yelled.

Country jumped when I yelled. When he saw me, he took the hammer into his left hand and yelled, "I'm gonna kill you, Torchy!" He then charged me. Busted hand or not, I knew not to tangle with him. I ran back into the bathroom, dropped the gym bag and immediately braced myself against the door. Country was huge and in a rage so I knew I couldn't hold him alone. I crowbarred myself up against the door and the shower wall.

BOOM! The first charge hit the door so hard my collarbone almost snapped in half. I saw drywall dust fly and one of the door screws flew across the room.

"I'm gonna kill you, Torchy!" Country yelled. "Embarrassing me like that!" BOOM! The next hit split the door and I heard something in my back pop. I had the wind knocked out of me, but I looked around for a weapon, and I saw Stephanie's Goofy toothbrush in a plastic cup on the sink.

BOOM! The next hit with such force, two door screws flew into the sink. Lights started popping around my eyes and my ears started ringing. I couldn't breathe. I dropped down, leapt for the sink and grabbed Steph's Goofy toothbrush just as Country smashed through the door.

Everything slowed down. As he flew through the door, I used the end of that Goofy toothbrush and shanked Country right in the ribs. He fishtailed in the air and grabbed at his side yelling, "He got me!" just as his head slammed into the toilet bowl.

I was hit with the half of the door and it caught my forehead, slicing me open. Blood immediately shot into my left eye, blinding me, and then I heard the crackle and pop of the fire coming closer. I could smell the carpets and drywall burning, and I knew that although I couldn't smell it, that urea foam from the couches was burning and cyanide gas was coming for us both.

My ribs. Something was wrong, sharp. It hurt to breathe. I reached around to see if something was inside me as I pushed the rest of the door aside and caught my reflection in the mirror. Blood was flowing pretty good. I had door chunks in my hair. I looked at Country and he was out cold. Fuck, my hand started to throb in the way only bone grinding on bone could. I wasn't stabbed. I had a broken rib or ribs.

"Son!" I heard a voice yell from outside through the open window in the shower. "Torchy!" It was Jeremiah.

"Son!" He called again. "Torchy—somebody answer me!" I held my breath and pain shot through my rib cage on my left. I wiped the blood away with my sleeve and took a quick look down the hall. There was a wall of fire coming at us. Black smoke started to fill the bathroom. I looked at Country and he was out. On his tummy and in la la land.

"Torchy! Is my son in there?" Jeremiah yelled. I had to think fast.

"Torchy—is my son in there? God! Jesus! Answer me!"

"He's in here!" I yelled, winced and pressed my good hand against my side. "Knocked out."

"You sonofabitch!" he yelled. "What'd you do to him? Your fuckin' trailer's on fire!" Thank fuck there was a side door. I looked at Country and I looked at the ten grand. There was no way I was going to go back for both. "Your stupid son threw a firebomb in the living room and he's knocked out!"

"Oh Lord. Torchy, you get him out of there right now. I'm begging you. She's burnin' up!" I knelt down so the smoke wouldn't blind my good eye. Blood started dripping in my mouth. The cyanide would be crawling along the floor, right into Country's mouth if I wasn't fast. I spit blood and looked at that gym bag of Sfen's and shook my head. *Shit!*

I grabbed Country by his ankles. "He knocked his own self out trying to kill me!"

"Torchy, you get my son out of there and I'll give you anything you want. You get him out of there, Torchy, and I promise you I'll give you anything." I could hear Jeremiah crying. "I swear to God, Torchy. I'll give you everything I have. I swear. Just give me my son back."

I took a big breath again and held it. I couldn't breathe or none of us would make it. I used my hands, despite the agony. And my shoulder was out—I knew it. I knew it. And though it killed me to do it, I pulled Country across the linoleum floor. Jesus Christ, it was like pulling solid cement. I opened the side door with my left hand and kicked open the cheap wooden door that opened onto the lawn. There was

no porch so it was about a three-foot drop. When Country's body
hit the carpet, he slowed down fast. I hopped out of the trailer and
pulled his ankles again, taking a big breath of what I thought would
be fresh air, but it was solid smoke. I started to cough and realized
that, with the carpet, there was no give in pulling Country. He was
too heavy. *Shit!* He was going to burn. That fire was racing over him,
licking at the furnace.

"Torchy!" Jeremiah yelled and I looked. Jeremiah stood with both
of his canes at the back of the trailer, too far away to help. "Where's
my son?"

"Help me!" I yelled. "He's too heavy!"

Jeremiah tried to run on the grass but he fell, spilling both canes
in front of him. *Shit!* I had to hop back in the trailer and push
Country out with my feet. There was fire everywhere now. Opening
that side door fed the fire and now it roared above Country. I heard
him moan. Which was worse because he'd feel everything when the
fire got him.

"Torchy, you save my son. Save my son!" Jeremiah yelled. He was
crying and crawling towards us. "I'm begging you! I'll give you anything you want!"

Half blinded by blood, I looked up and saw an arm of fire shoot
out of the roof. And the roar of it being fed by air created a wind. I
took the biggest breath I could but coughed when it felt like I had a
bag of nails in my right lung. I coughed and wiped blood out of my
eye and I saw the whole front end of the trailer engulfed in the red-
dest fire I ever saw. Black smoke filled the sky and the siding was starting to pop.

I took a shallow breath and jumped back into the trailer, through
the smoke and cyanide gas and smashed my head hard into the gyproc.
Stars. I saw stars but I knew not to breathe. And then I felt it.

The wind.

The same wind I felt around Snowbird that day. It surrounded
me. Time slowed. I seen a blue light shimmering above Country's

body. It was in a bright blue I'd never seen before, and blue strings of light braided themselves together like tendrils out of Country's nose and mouth starting to make their way towards the ceiling. I blinked and looked closer. The strings were getting thicker and whatever it was — his spirit? — was reaching higher. Then I heard hissing. I turned and saw black fingers crawling along the floor from the hallway. It was the cyanide gas and it was coming for his mouth. I blinked and crawled over Country's body. I dropped fast against the wall and, with all my might, I kicked his body out of the trailer. He barely moved. So I did it again, this time planting my feet against his ribs and I booted with everything I had. He was gone in a second and I saw light reach through the smoke towards me.

Then I felt the full heat of the fire engulf me. I heard a roar of the wind around me and my hair went up with a *whoosh!* I started slapping the flames away. Sfen's shirt went up and that's when I jumped with all I had into the light. I hit hard, jamming my thumb on my broken hand. The agony kept me alert as I knew I was on fire.

"Jesus Christ!" someone yelled.

"He's on fire!" someone yelled. I was beside Country and could hear sirens and people racing towards me. It was my neighbours. I felt my back starting to burn and I immediately started to roll on the grass over and over. Over and over. Over and over until I was jumped by someone with a blanket. I was told later it was Glen Holmes, manager of the Northern. I was also told I tried choking him out, even when I was unconscious.

All I know is I remember Jeremiah holding Country like a baby. Jeremiah couldn't stop crying and Country kept calling, "Thank you, Torchy. I'm sorry, Torchy."

I was on my stomach on a stretcher, breathing into an oxygen tank and coughing tar out something awful. My ribs hurt and my shoulder was killing me. The ambulance guys put an ice pack on my eye and wouldn't let me look at my hand. Everything hurt: my back, my hand, my eye, my lungs and my scalp, ears and forehead were killing me. I didn't even feel the gash on my forehead. I had been on fire. Apparently, I flew like the Human Torch out of Sfen's trailer, onto Sfen's lawn. A fricken Dogrib Evel Knievel on fire, no less....

The hospital wasn't too bad. When I woke, it felt like I'd been sucking on a blood popsicle for a month. I'd bit halfway through my tongue somewhere along the way and it was swollen. I could handle my stitches and broken hand easy with my meds, but I had this wicked cough and second degree burns on my shoulders. It turns out Country broke three of my ribs and dislocated my shoulder. He also cracked my collarbone. I could feel all my torn muscles every time I breathed so I learned how to breathe slow. The nurses had given me a pig shave as I guess my hair had gone up in the fire and that was fine with me. Me and Sfen always had pig shaves when we were kids and it was nice to have some air conditioning blowing on my neck and ears.

I had visitors, believe it or not. The old man and Stephanie were by my side for the full three days I was there, only leaving when guests came. I kept waiting for Arnie to be admitted, but, strangely, there was no sign of him. Lester's mother came to visit. I was still on my stomach, unable to sit up fully or lie on my side. She brought me a patch quilt blanket she'd made herself.

"Thank you for spending time with Lester before he passed." I nodded, taking shallow breaths. "I was able to speak to Lester before he died," she said, "and he told me he'd asked you to do a few things before he passed."

I was tired but wanted to do this right. "I did everything he asked," I said. "I'm sorry I didn't get back in time."

"He knows," she said and smiled. She looked tired.

"I'm sorry," I said, "that I was such a bully to him."

She nodded. "He said you became his biggest protector."

I nodded. "I looked out for him as best I could."

She smiled. "Someone wants to thank you, too." I looked. She motioned towards the door and Charity walked into the room.

"Hi, Torchy," she said.

"Hi," I nodded.

"Everyone's saying you're a hero." That's when I saw Lester's cross around her neck.

I took a big breath and winced. "I sure don't feel like one."

Charity looked at Lester's mom and looked at me. "You're going to be an uncle."

"What?"

"I'm going to be a grandmother," Lester's mom said. There were tears in her eyes. "And you're going to be an uncle."

I looked at Charity and she had the biggest smile on her face. "We're going to raise Lester's son and we'd like you to help—as family."

I nodded. "Holy fuck. Deal." I started to cough and faded into sleep.

After that, Jeremiah and Country came to visit. They walked in with their caps in their hands and the biggest puppy dog eyes I ever seen.

"I'm sorry for busting you up and burning your brother's trailer," Country said. I saw Jeremiah wipe his eyes. "Thank you for saving my life. Are you okay?"

"I will be," I said. I then started to cough and they looked at each other with panic. I'm sure it hurt worse than I put on but my meds were kicking in just fine.

"Can I get you anything?" Country asked.

"No," I said. "They say I gotta cough it all up. It's okay."

Jeremiah caned his way towards me, with Country helping him out. "Listen, Torchy. The RCMP are asking questions. They have a fire expert in from Yellowknife and they're waiting to talk to you."

"So?" I asked.

"Maybe we can work out a little deal." Sfen's trailer was gone. All our stuff was gone. Stephanie's Goofy toothbrush was gone. The ten grand was gone. My brother's Bible.

"I want you to know, Torchy—and I swear to God on this—that when we moved your brother's body we used respect. We did rebury him next to your mother's resting place. And we feel bad you lost your brother's trailer."

I thought of him and Jeremiah taking Sfen's body out of the earth and moving it, disturbing his peace. I didn't have the strength to get angry or tell them off so I just listened. "Go on."

"I built a new house near the highway. It's my best design yet. Four rooms, big yard, picture windows. You name it. It was supposed to be for the new doctor but I told the hospital I'd build them another one. Torchy," he said and held out the keys, "it's all yours." I looked at it. I knew which one he was talking about. It was a beauty all right. No expense had been spared. I couldn't believe it.

"But," Jeremiah said, "I want your word that you'll clear my son's name when you speak to the police."

"I lost that ten grand," I said.

"What?" they asked.

"After the fight, I went to my brother's to clean up when Country firebombed the trailer. It was either you, Country, or the ten grand. It all went up in the flames."

"No way," Jeremiah said. "I think that house more than covers—"

"You promised me," I said, "that if I saved your son's life, you'd give me anything I wanted. His biggest claim to fame is he's never been put down, right? Well, you cut me a cheque for ten grand and I won't tell UFC if you don't."

Country looked at his father and his father looked at his son. Jeremiah teared up and hugged his son again. "Done," he said and he asked his son to go to the truck and get his chequebook.

When Country left, Jeremiah stood over me, looking at the gauze on my back and checking out my cast. "Is our war over?"

I looked at him and my back began to sting. "You dug up my brother's body."

He nodded. "True, but you have to believe me that we moved him with respect and dignity. I buried him the way every Dogrib should be buried. And I got him away from the wolves, Torchy. They'd been trying. Believe me. I swear it on my son's life. That was no way for anyone to be buried." I could hear that he was telling the truth.

"I think we've done enough to each other, don't you?" he asked.

"You promise me on your son's life you buried him beside our mother?" I asked.

He nodded. "I swear. I swear on everything, Torchy. Your brother is buried right beside your mother. Where he should be. And we can even help make a crib to surround it. We can wait a year to do it. Dogrib style."

I thought about it. I thought about my beautiful brother. His strong hands. The way he'd touch my back when he walked by. "Our war is over," I said and started to cough.

Jeremiah caned his way over to me and gently put his hand on my left wrist. "Thank you for saving my son's life."

I nodded. His big hand trembled and I could tell he was choking up. "I have something for you," he said. He placed something in my hands and closed my fingers around it. "Get well, Torchy."

I looked at what he gave me and it was a rosary. The rosary we stole from the warden. The rosary Sfen held as he pulled the trigger. The rosary he'd been buried and dug up with.

"Jesus," I said. I started to tear up. I missed my brother terribly and even my mom. Whenever they'd let me out of here, we'd have to have a ceremony.

After Country came back, Jeremiah signed his cheque to me.

"Thank you," I said.

"No," he said. "Thank you."

"Should I ask about Arnie?" I asked.

"Oh," Jeremiah said, "he's been taken care of." I frowned but knew not to ask another word. I then asked them for a favour.

Talking to the cops was a cinch. I told them Country had come over asking me for help. His dad had run out of gas and he didn't want to walk out to the highway himself. I said we'd gone outside to look for a funnel and when we came back it was my cigarette that did the trailer in. They just shook their heads and left it at that.

What nobody knows, and what I'll never tell, is after Jeremiah and Country came to see me, and after the cops left, my brother's ex—Andy the fire chief—paid me a visit. He brought with him what looked like a dirty oil rag in a baggy. "You're lucky you made it out of that fire alive," he said.

"How's that?" I asked.

"We figure she went up in about three minutes."

"It felt shorter than that."

"I bet." He nodded. "Is this your shirt?"

I looked at it. It was hard to believe but it was. "It was Sfen's."

He looked at it and I could tell he wanted to touch it. "What I don't understand," he said, "is the shirt went up like this and you only got burnt on your shoulders. You're one lucky man."

I nodded. "I know."

"Tell your brother when you see him," he said, "that I said—"

"He's dead," I said.

Andy took in a big breath as if gut punched. "What?" he asked.

"He's gone," I said and I told Andy everything. Oh, how he cried. Andy cried and cried. Snowbird would check on us but he knew to stand by and send other visitors away. When we were done, I told Andy what we intended to do with Sfen's remains and he told me he'd be there. He then pulled something out from where he'd put his jacket. Because I was on my stomach, I couldn't see it.

"A gym bag," he said. "Filled with a pile of money. And a Bible."

I smiled. "No way."

He nodded. "It was in the tub. I'm amazed it didn't burn. We put that fire out and that's the only thing that made it." He put it beside me.

"In the tub?" I asked. "Last time I saw it she was by the sink."

He shrugged. "All I know is you earned it," he said. "Every penny. We watched you fight and man, that was something. Nobody on my crew knows about this, and your secret's safe with me."

I looked at him. "And your secret's safe with me."

He nodded. "Thank you, Torchy. Thank you." *One stair closer to heaven,* I thought. *But how did that bag get in the tub? Sfen? Snowbird?* I know I felt Snowbird's wind before my hair went up, but I couldn't believe it. Maybe the good Lord above was finally taking a shine to me.

Last but not least was Snowbird. Stephanie went to get a juice in the pop machine and the old man stood by my bed. "Sorry Lester didn't make it," he said.

"Yeah."

"He was a good boy," he said softly. "Where did they bury your brother?" he asked.

"Right next to my mom," I said.

Just then, Stephanie came skipping into the room with her juice. "You're a hero, Torchy. Did you find my Goofy toothbrush?"

"Sorry, baby girl," I said. "It went up in the fire, but it saved my life."

"What?"

"I'll tell you about it some day, okay?"

"Sure, but you owe me a new one."

I smiled. "Okay."

"Aunty says she'd like to make us all supper when you're better."

I smiled. "Sounds good to me."

Snowbird sniffed and sneezed. "What's burnt?"

I looked at the gym bag and at the cheque Jeremiah signed for me. "You won't believe me if I tell you."

Snowbird put his hands on mine. "Try me."

Jeremiah and his boys had done a good job of replanting the bodies and coffins of the previous townies of Fort Simmer. There were new pine crosses on every grave I could see. To the left were a pile of old rotted-out white crosses that were off to the dump to get burned.

The family crosses of some of the biggest townie families were grouped together: the Snuffs, the Otters, the Red Hats. My brother and mother were buried together at the very south of the boneyard.

On my way there, I saw a lot of "In God We Trust-s," "Loved By All Who Knew Him-s," and an "Our Pride and Joy." To my surprise, I remembered after Mom died, Sfen and I carved "We love you Mom" into the back of her cross, but I saw it had been replaced by a new pine one. And right next to it was Sfen's.

I hadn't been here in years. Last time was on my eighteenth birthday when I got good and drunk and told my mother I hated her for leaving us. I cried. Oh I cried, but then I told her how good Sfen was doing, how hard he was working to get his business going, and I kept quiet about me. I didn't want her to know about how I'd turned and started my own private war with God for all He took from me. I told her that if I did go to hell, I'd see my father there and finally know who he was. For I was a product of rape. I was the son of force and take.

So much taken, so much lost. So much pain and misery. But that would be another story. Right now, here we were, on a beautiful day. Snowbird and Stephanie were to my right. Jeremiah and Country were to my left. I had only been here once before sober and that was to watch the gravediggers put my mom in the earth after she died. Sfen had been with me and we had cried so pitifully together. That was the day we promised to look after each other no matter what.

Trucks had been cruising by since we got here, slowing down and watching. I didn't care. Some trucks stopped. Others sped up to spread the news. I was sure that more trucks would be coming as word spread. For some reason, I was picking up Gunner strong and fierce. I had a feeling he and I weren't done with each other yet and, when I was stronger, I'd deal with him and that nail gun situation. He kept jumping into his punches and it was always so easy to time my strikes, but that would be later: another time, another place.

Snowbird began singing a soft song, one that brought tears to my eyes. I watched him move and drop tobacco to each of the four directions. He looked sharp, dressed in new clothes. So did Stephanie in her pretty summer dress. I stood in some new duds and I had to smile. My cast was so big I had to cut the arm off my new shirt to get it on. But there we were honouring my brother's new resting place, and my mother not being alone on the other side. It was a beautiful day to say goodbye.

I don't know where she learned this, but Stephanie had cut three ribbons for each of us. They were red. She'd pinned them with little clothespins to our shirts and they looked sharp.

Off in the distance, a horde of about twenty kids on bikes sped by yelling but stopped when they saw Snowbird dropping tobacco. The leader pointed with his chin to our group and all twenty of them turned to get a closer look. One wrong move from any of them and I'd be over that fence so fast it'd make their heads spin.

Nothing.

They all watched in awe as the old man blessed my brother and my mother and I saw two of the boys take their caps off in respect for our gathering. Maybe there was hope for our future yet. I looked east and there was Andy sitting in his truck, watching from a safe distance. I knew in the south our new house stood waiting for us to have a feast after, and what a house it was. I had buried ten thousand dollars in the backyard. The move hadn't cost a lot, but buying grub and clothes for everyone hadn't been cheap.

Snowbird, Country and Jeremiah were invited back to the house after the funeral. They promised to help build picket fences for Sfen and Mom's graves in a year, as was the Dogrib custom. I told Andy he could bring his wife if he wanted to visit.

But here, in this place, lay my brother and my mother.

I could hear an ATV zipping around in the distance, and I saw a jet flying overhead. I was about to trance out when Snowbird looked at me and handed me some tobacco. I took some, took it to my nose and inhaled before dropping it softly on the earth. It was then a full wave of sadness got me.

"Sfen, my brother, you left too soon," I said and started to cry. "You were buried Dogrib-style with your feet closest to the cross. This way you could pull yourself up to the sky. You can soar to heaven, brother."

The last time we were here was the last time I cried, and I am crying now, years of hate and steam and hurt and the cocaine gland discharging like invisible trumpets, all let loose, all set free. I'm reaching for your hand.

You were too young, so impossibly beautiful to die like you did, and I've always pretended you were on a trip, somewhere, never too far away and you'd call, you'd write, you'd show up when I was sleeping and we'd go. We'd go wherever you wanted and I'd cook for you, make you coffee, bring it to you in the sunrise or late afternoon and we'd laugh, like brothers, like sons together and you'd be there for me. Isn't that the promise every big brother makes?

"You're safe now, Sfen." I listen to Steph read the Bible and the words bring comfort. They blanket us. I lean into those words as they rise and rise and I'll never stop loving you no....

The Contract

WE STAND OUTSIDE THE PRINCIPAL'S HOUSE WHERE WENDY WAS raped. I can smell the river grass and winter's on her way. Here I am again, this time with an ally.

"What's the name of this ceremony?" he asks.

I hold the last rat root I was ever given by my ehtsi and light the end until it starts to smoke by itself.

"Blessing Wendy," I say.

In my Ninja side sack were the ways I was going to kill the principal when he came back for court. I had a hundred yards of nylon fishing wire I could see through. And I had red spider venom.

I had stolen the venom from the doctor who used it for a wart on my thumb. The shaving and peeling with a razor and then attacking the wart with liquid nitrogen for the past three months hadn't worked, so he'd brought out the ultimate wart remover.

"If this doesn't work," he said, "nothing will." He touched my wart with the end of a toothpick laced with the venom for a full second. Four hours later my thumb swelled to twice its size. I thought for a week that my thumb had become egg filled with thousands of red spiders, ready to burst out if I pressed down too hard. My entire arm felt as if I'd been Hiroshima-flashburned and my shirt had melted through my skin. But it worked. It worked so well that when I went back to the clinic for a check-up, I stole the bottle, and now no scar remains. None.

My wish was to burn the principal from the inside out alive in his sleep. I was going to find him, open his sunroof wherever he slept, lower the fish wire over his snoring mouth and drip the stolen venom down his throat. He would gag to death on fire.

The wart had come from the same locker room where Marvin, two days after he arrived and began beating us all at break, walked out of the shower naked (the only boy in the history of PWS to ever *use* the shower) and said, "That's right, boys. Have a good look. Most of youse don't have hair number one yet, but I got more than all of youse put together."

It was true: hair on his face, chin, sideburn, chest, nuts, balls, man fur. His cock hung curved and darker than the rest of him. His was a man's cock in a room full of boys — boys who changed quickly under towels from home, boys who'd rather go to class with sweaty asses and dink grease from their own musk glands than shower and change.

"That's right," he smiled and looked around. I hated his yellow spike teeth and the shadow of his mustache. "I've already gone through puberty, and I already had my first period." Half the room started laughing while the others got up and left, only to burst out laughing outside the room.

When Barnes walked Marvin into the class and announced he'd been transferred from Fort Smith, I knew Marvin was trouble. He was taller than all of us and he was built like a man. I sniffed the air and could smell something sweet and high from him.

All suspicions were confirmed when he started beating us all, especially me. And there were no teachers anywhere. Another staff meeting, I guess, to deal with what the principal left behind.

"Hey, harelip," Marvin said as he came up behind me to give me a kidney shot. The pain broke me. My legs gave and I dropped my side sack. I crouched, then collapsed, shouldering my own weight into my locker. Dizzy with pain, my stomach rolled. I started breathing out of my nose as Marvin curled his lips back. "Tomorrow you'll bring me a pack of Export A's. King size."

He wound up to knuckle my face. "Okay?" I nodded, speechless from pain, held my hand up and fell to the floor. Brian and his posse turned the corner towards us at the worst possible second. Brian was gorgeous. The white wolf. Marvin dismissed me and charged, an ape charging a wolf pack.

"Hey—" was all Brian could say before Marvin attacked. Brian's pack of four fanned out and ran from the doors. Marvin hit him a lot harder than he hit me and Brian held his chest and started to cry. Marvin whispered an order into Brian's ear, and Brian nodded and sobbed before Marvin charged out the door.

It took me a while, but I pulled myself up. I grabbed my side sack and my Book of Plans and put it in my locker. I felt like a pack of huskies had attacked me and my legs were tingling. When I went to see if Brian was okay, he looked at me and looked away. "Fuck off," he said. I did.

Next day, Marvin was the king. He chain-smoked and slurped Dr. Pepper and counted his cash. He kept digging into his ear with his free hand and that's when I noticed that the toque he wore to class was actually quite stinky. I wrote, "Marvin's wearing a toque in class" on a piece of paper and left it on Barnes's desk. He read it as he was taking attendance.

"Marvin," Barnes looked up from his note. "Hats off to education."

"What?" Marvin said. Everyone sat up.

"You're new here, but we have a school policy that applies to all students." His eyes fluttered like dragonfly wings as they always do when he's nervous and he pointed to Marvin's head. "Hats off."

Marvin looked around. Bruised and stinging, we glared at him. "I got a doctor's note," he said. "Ear infection. I got to keep them covered." He pulled out an orange pill container from his breast pocket and shook it. The pills sounded plastic as they rolled around in the container. There were lots of them.

"Fine," Barnes said and folded my note into his pocket without looking around. "Let's get back to work."

Ninety percent of assassination is gathering information, so after school I raced home and asked Rob, the house parent of the Northern Leaders program, "Tell me everything you know about ear infections." I pulled out my Book of Plans and took notes, lots of them. And true to Rob's words, Marvin's strength faded as every day I trained harder. I was doing push-ups, pull-ups, crunches and stretches.

I waited for Brian at his locker. For once he was alone. His pack of four were probably smoking by the swimming pool. In the past, Brian's ignored me. I know he's made fun of me at the bush parties but I didn't care. "You're in my way," he said and went around me.

"We can hurt him," I said.

He started doing his combination. "Who?"

I wanted to cover my lips with my hand, but I looked away. I couldn't look at his lips or teeth. They were too beautiful. "I, uh, know how to get Marvin."

Brian stopped. "How?"

Sensing weakness, we waited a whole day. I asked to go to the washroom and was given the nod by Mr. Kenny. I went through Marvin's locker and horked all over Marvin's pills before adding a little bit of water and placing the lid back tightly. Marvin wasn't Treaty so he had to pay for his meds, and it didn't look like he was rich. I came back and nodded to Brian who then nodded to his pack. They all nodded back to me, wolves nodding to a bear.

Marvin didn't even check his pill container when he changed. He didn't mention a thing the next day at school, but I saw him peeking around, searching for a giveaway in the eyes from the one who ambushed his meds.

"What do you think?" Brian asked at my locker.

"Not yet," I said.

"You sure?"

I nodded. "Positive." There were a few more beatings from Marvin for the few kids too slow to sprint away at break but his reign was over. Brian and his pack walked in groups to their classes. I patrolled and watched Marvin lean hard against the walls at break, looking up at the lights, weak from sickness inside his skull.

Marvin's stink became rotten. Pus leaked from his ears. He wore his toques to class to cover this, mop the drainage up and hold it. *This was it.*

I ran by Brian at lunch. "Now."

"You sure?" he asked.

"Positive. Call your pack!" I dropped my side sack and ran behind Marvin who was limping home and kicked his leg out from behind him. He buckled and collapsed.

I turned and Brian led his pack. "Come on!" he yelled. "Get him!" My job was done. Brian pushed me out of the way and the crew took over.

"My ear's infected!" Marvin cried as we laid the boots to him. "No fair!"

The pack had him. Shane and Barry took his legs. Tony and Marcel took his arms. They looked at me. Brian yelled, "Get him, Bear! He hit you first."

I sniffed the air. I could smell the high, electric buzz of terror. I began to breathe through my mouth and swerve my head. My neck bristled and I made claws with my fingers. I showed my teeth, incisor to incisor.

"What the fuck are you?" Marvin screamed.

Horror spread across the faces of Brian and his crew. I began to look this way and that, licking my lips quickly. "I'm a bear," I whispered and ran my tongue over my teeth. I ran, jumped and brought my curled fist down on his balls again and again while he kicked and bucked.

"Yeah!" Tony cried.

"Fuck him up!"

"Get him, Bear. Sic him!" I attacked and mauled and roared through my bear lips.

I blurred out and saw my grandma. She had a harelip too. She pointed to her lip and then to mine and said, "Sah" which means "bear." They say she had bear medicine, just like Wendy.

"Whoah! Whoah! Hey!" Brian yelled and grabbed me. I was punching Marvin so hard in the balls I could feel the coiled root of nerves at the base of his scrotum. I had punched through his balls. The boys who'd been holding his legs apart had stopped and were pulling me off.

"Cool it, man," Tony said. "The new VP's coming."

I looked, cleared my eyes, snorted. The new vice-principal was coming all right, but not in any hurry. He was smoking and walking leisurely towards us. He knew Marvin deserved this.

I could hear sobbing and looked down. Marvin held his nuts and rolled slowly back and forth.

"Now boys—" the VP said.

"Fuck you!" Marvin cried out suddenly. "I'll kill all of youse!"

The VP put his hands on his hips and assessed the damage. "What happened here?"

Tony pointed to Marvin. "Marvin's been bullying us since he's been here."

I didn't need to listen. I started to walk away. I grabbed my side sack and made sure my Book of Plans was inside. I looked back only once and saw nothing but pride in Brian's eyes. Marvin's reign of terror had only lasted a week. He was fuck-all now. Word was out: if you dropped him, you could hurt him. And you could take your time doing that.

To my surprise, Brian called me that night.

"How you doing?"

"Good."

"What you doing this Friday?"

"Not much."

"We were wondering if you would like to come to my house. My folks'll be out of town."

I couldn't say no. This was what I wanted. I had earned something today and maybe it was time for me to not be different anymore. If they accepted me, the school would accept me. "Okay."

"See you at ten," he said and then he hung up.

The sad thing after the mauling was that after that you could nudge Marvin and he'd topple. He had no balance anymore. The students now dropped him for sport. When he did show up for class, he'd stay late after school, begging to do his homework in the library with the detention kids while a small pack of former victims waited to down him outside.

I went to Brian's locker to wait for him, but felt stupid, waiting there like a puppy, so I left. Neither him nor his crew said a word to me Wednesday or Thursday.

After the principal was captured in Calgary, he was charged for abusing Wendy. He's supposed to come back for his trial this month. Once it made the paper, people seemed to move in slow motion everywhere I looked. They closed the school for three days, made the vice-principal the principal and hired a woman from the south to help out. They brought in counsellors for the students. I played hooky for a week and nobody called.

I remembered Wendy with her own medicine. When we still lived in Rae, Ehtsi took us out to Trapper's Point. *She had the feeling.* Her palms were burning. Gran showed us both what bear root looks like and asked us to find some while she pretended to pick cranberries. I went into the clearing first and came back empty-handed. Wendy went in and returned with an armful.

"Bear root is what the bears love," Ehtsi said. "It's medicine for the heart. It can clear arteries and make the heart muscles strong, but she only shows herself to a few." So the root blossomed because it knew Wendy was coming near.

Most times — well, sometimes — whenever I'd see Wendy at school, I'd say hi. "Hi hi," she'd say and squealed with joy. It was like she couldn't contain the life inside her. She was a kid really. Her black Dogrib hair to her shoulders, her big Dogrib eyes, that big Dogrib smile. The teachers had to watch her because she was so friendly. She'd want to run to wherever the most students were. She wanted to play.

And with a body like hers, no one wants to play with you anymore. They want to fuck and feel and finger.

But our Shiver Ceremony—when we knew we were moving to Simmer for school, we knew we had to break her to trust me and only me. Standing in the abandoned DPW warehouse, we tied glass Coke bottles to fishing lines. There were eight of us boys, five of whom were cousins. We brought her in and she was scared. Wendy stood in the light. Looking down. Feet turned in. Alone.

I walked into the light in front of her and held my hand out. "Wendy," I said. "*Zunchlei*. Come." The boys shifted in the shadows. Luke coughed and I was scared she'd bolt. Once she started running it was so hard to catch her. She tried stepping left. "Hi hi." And the boy closest to her started shivering his fishing rod quickly, so that Coke bottle rattled. Then the other boys did it. *Tukkatukkatukkatukkatukka.*

The place sounded haunted with eight poles shivering their Coke bottles and she didn't like the sound. I was worried she'd flee, but she stepped towards me and they stopped. She looked around and stepped to the right, and the boys started again with the Shiver Ceremony—*tukkatukkatukkatukkatukka*—and she stepped towards me and we were quiet.

"Come, Wendy," I said. "It's me. I'm your cousin, Bear—remember?" And she ran to me quickly and hugged. We did this for seven days. That's how we broke her. To me.

The longer school went on the less she showed up. I never asked why. I was too busy living my bullshit life here. A town Indian. Like a white.

I do know that the teachers had to watch her for a reason. Her body. That trust. That everything inside her was just bursting to get out. You could do anything to her and she'd never tell. She was working on her words, but she was still like a baby.

So there I was, outside of Brian's house. It was like a castle it was so big. I could hear the bass inside and laughter from an open window.

Could I really fit in here? With my torn face and my shy ways. I held my Ninja side sack as the smell of town filled my nostrils—

"Whatcha doin'?" someone asked. I looked. It was Marvin. In the path by Brian's driveway. His toque was still on and he was having a smoke while he straddled his bike. In a second, I knew: he was waiting for someone, anyone, to see him outside Brian's and invite him in. He was lonely.

"Hey," I said.

"What you doin' there?" he asked again.

"Brian invited me to a party."

He looked at me suspiciously. "A freak party? That must be the same party he invited me to when I first moved here." I looked at him.

He shook his head. "How fuckin' retarded." He spat. "They trick you. They either get you to play seven minutes in heaven with one of the girls and she tells them everything after or they get you drunk and leave you naked somewhere."

"So what did they do with you?" I ask.

He shook his head. "My dad told me about it just in time."

Shit! I thought. I knew he was speaking the truth. I would never fit in. Ever. "Why are you here?"

"Cruising. You're psycho, hey?"

I nod. "Can be. Yeah."

"Wanna cruise?" he asked suddenly.

I relaxed and looked into his eyes. *Fuck it.* "Okay."

"Get on." I did. We doubled and raced through town.

"Where do you go at night?" Marvin asked me.

"What?"

"I've been tracking you. Why do you go to that house?"

I'm shocked. *Tracking or hunting?* "My cousin was raped there."

"She's the one, huh?"

"What?"

"The one who was raped. Everyone's hush-hush about it. She was your cousin?"

"Yeah."

"My sister died when I was five. I still remember that. So what do you do there?"

"I bless it."

"With what?"

"Light." I tapped the middle of his ribs and that felt wonderful. "From here." *I pray with my body* is what I'm trying to say.

"What the fuck?" Marvin stops pedalling, and I look ahead. Here, six kids walk towards us staring straight ahead.

"Children of the corn, or what?" he asked. The children walk towards us quietly and I'm speechless. I put my feet on the ground to balance the bike. They come towards us and one boy leads the pack.

"Hey, you little shit monkeys," Marvin says. "What's going on?" The leader raises his right hand and it's covered in blood.

"Holy shit," Marvin says.

I look at the rest of the kids and their hands are covered in it. "What are you kids up to?" I ask.

The boy looks at me. "Orders from Torchy and Sfen," he says. "Leave your mark on any house you've been touched or raped in. They'll take care of the rest."

"Sfen and Torchy," Marvin says. "The dog killers?"

The boy nods. "Use red paint or blood."

"For what?" I ask.

"We do what we're told," he looks back at the group. "Let's go." The group move on without a word and I see as they pass they have packsacks. One of the kids is carrying a bucket of red paint.

"Freaky," Marvin says. I watch them leave. "Sfen and Torchy. I heard they're bad news."

"They love being dog killers a bit too much." He looked east. "Wanna see a cool hiding place?"

"Sure."

"Let's go." Marvin doubled me to the high school and ditched his bike behind a wall of fibreglass. They must have been doing renovations up top. We climbed the huge pink pillows of fibreglass. They were the perfect stairs to the roof.

"Hurry," he says. "Cops patrol by all the time." We climb. We're up in no time. We sit up top where it's cool. "It'll be dusk all night," Marvin said, looking over the town.

"Ever smoke up?" he asked.

I nod. "Not in a long time."

"Do you believe what I said about them tricking you?"

I look around: there's the water tower with the red light at the top blinking away. I nod. "Yeah."

"You were deceived by wolves." There's the church steeple. There's the hockey arena.

"Read the latest *National Geographic*?"

"Nope."

"It says wolves are born knowing not to trust strangers."

"Why?"

"They're pack animals. They can't afford to trust anyone outside of their own."

I nod. Luke and I used to be like that. "You're smart, hey?"

"Have to be," he said. "Dad's a cop."

"No way." He nods. I let my breath drain from my lungs.

"I could use a friend," he said. "I think you could too."

We look at each other sideways. He's right. "I'm sorry about your sister," I say.

He nods. "Sorry about your cousin." He pulls out a small pipe and takes out a bag. Looks like weed. He makes preparations and I can see the town. I squint and see that on the water tower, someone's painted Grad 2012 already on the sides in huge letters—

"Well, well," a voice says from the darkness behind us.

I jump and look. From the shadows step Torchy and Sfen. Banned for life from school. Banned for life from every bar in town—and they're not even legal yet. Shit. My spider venom is in my side sack and I have four sticks of rat root in my pocket—

"What do we have here?" Sfen asks as they surround us. Marvin is holding his breath, sitting very still. I can't meet their eyes. I'm scared by what I feel from them.

"It's a Tlicho and a whitey," Torchy says. "How cute." They have us.

"Lucky for you," Sfen says. "We're Dogrib, too. What you got there?"

Torchy took Marvin's dope and sniffed the bag. "Oh dear," he said. "Someone's sold you oregano. This is not grass."

"For shame." Sfen swiped the bag and the pipe away. "Was your dealer Kevin Garner?" Marvin nodded.

"Tell you what," Torchy said before we could answer. "We'll talk to him for you and make sure you are compensated for this obvious miscommunication."

"Look likes that boy needs to be taught," Sfen agreed.

Torchy snickered. "Sometimes a small town boot fuck reminds us of what is important." Sfen took out his own bag and sprinkled something on the pipe and began to light up. Torchy gripped my shoulder hard. His grip was iron. I saw a cross tattooed across the length of his forearms. I couldn't read the writing on it but it said something. "Is it true the young girl that principal raped was one of us?"

I nodded.

"Any relation to you?" he asked. His grip grew harder.

"My cousin," I said.

His grip softened. I could hear Marvin dry swallow beside me. "Any relation to my brother and me?"

I looked. "You're Dogrib? What are you doing here?"

"Answer the question. Was she any relation to us?"

"Who's your mom?" I asked and there was power in this. Maybe this would save us. Sfen spoke their mother's name, and I knew of her family. They were from Snare Lakes, Wekweti. In my mind I touched the branches on the family tree. "Wendy was your second cousin."

Torchy dropped his hand and looked at his brother who whistled. "Is it true she needed surgery after he raped her?"

The question floored me. Tears came to my eyes. "Yes."

Torchy let all of his breath out and looked at the night sky. He closed his eyes hard and swallowed. I saw his eyelids tremble and his face harden with a decision.

Sfen looked at Marvin. "Is whitey with you?"

I looked at Marvin who was frozen with fear. "Yes."

Torchy leaned into him and spat on Marvin's shoe. "Lucky bitch."

Sfen lit the pipe again and thought for a while. "Let us not be enemies," he inhaled.

"We know who the true enemy is now," Torchy agreed. He held the pipe above his head and took a drag. He then handed me the pipe. "I wanna see your breath to know you ain't lyin'." I gulped and looked around. Torchy and Sfen were watching me intently. Marvin stared at his shoes. I took a hit and the smoke filled my mouth like murder. I was immediately blown over by an invisible snowplow. My soul shot out of my body, up into the sky, way past the faint feathers of the growing northern lights and I swirled around for a bit. I fell so carefully down into my body that when I came back I had to sit down. I couldn't even hand the pipe to Marvin. Torchy did it for me.

Marvin took a hoot and looked down. "Whoah," he said. "Whoah."

"Kevin Garner may have sold you oregano," Sfen said, "but he deals good coke."

"What is this?" I asked.

Sfen handed the pipe back to me and smiled. "Good medicine."

Torchy and Sfen walked up to me and knelt down. Torchy lit a smoke. "You're new here, so listen up. You can trust the Slavey, maybe the Gwich'in and the Hare, but stay away from the Chipewyan and the Crees."

"Chipewyan are famous for being jealous," Sfen said.

"And Crees are always horny," Torchy warned.

"Yeah," Sfen said, "this ain't their land but they want it."

"It's all buddy-buddy until the back alley," Torchy said.

Torchy walked up to Marvin and blew smoke in his face. "They say they got the first part of Indian country with the bottle and the second half with the Bible." He looked at me and pulled out a long knife. He then looked at Marvin. Marvin's eyes widened and he froze. "And never trust the whites. Look at what happened to our cousin."

Marvin started to kick and whimper and Torchy made the motion of slicing him slowly up and down in the sign of the cross. The last slash would be across the throat, and I yelled, "Wait!" Torchy stopped and saw my hand held out with three of the four sticks of rat root. He motioned to Sfen to go see.

Sfen walked up to me, knelt down and carefully picked up the three rat roots I carried since being here. "Brother," he said. "Medicine from home."

"Na," Torchy said. "Let's see." Sfen handed the gnarled roots to his brother who sniffed them. They both looked at me with respect. Torchy nodded. Sfen did too.

"You stole my dope," Marvin said suddenly. Both Torchy and Sfen were surprised by his courage.

"Better than your ass cherry," Sfen said and the brothers snickered. They then motioned to each other and Sfen handed me the pipe. "We're telling everyone we meet to leave a red handprint on any house you've been touched or raped in. Do it before the principal comes back for his trial."

"Why?" Marvin asked.

Torchy looked at Marvin and shook his head. "Never you mind, buttercup." Torchy looked back once and held up Marvin's dope. "Fair trade for the rat root, eh?"

The brothers then jumped off the roof and vanished. Marvin and I were quiet for a very long time. I was kind of floating and falling at the same time.

"What the fuck was that?" Marvin asked with his eyes closed.

"Magic," I said.

"They stole my dope," Marvin said. I was rolling backwards within my own body, just circling and circling within my own shell. *Better than your ass cherry*, I wanted to say and then I started to giggle.

"What did you give them?"

I tried being serious. Why were my hands tingling? "Rat root."

"What?"

"One of the five most powerful roots in the world."

"What does it do?"

"It saves lives." Then I burst out laughing.

"Oh. Hey. You said you were a bear," Marvin says. He's smiling, dizzy eyed. "Say more about this."

I smirk. "You're stoned."

He shrugged and smiled. "I confess that I am."

It tasted like someone put a light bulb in my mouth and turned it on. I started to cough. There was no spit left on my tongue. "A bear always knows what you're thinking."

He nodded. "I understand." Then he, too, started laughing.

I giggled in spurts. "A bear is blind for three days after he claws his way out of his den in the spring."

We started laughing together. I turned to him and he aged in front of me. I saw a handsome man instead of a bully. "The words you say are wise," he giggled. "Who taught you?"

"My gran." I suddenly sense there is a tap somewhere on this roof. I start looking for it. I really need to drink something—now.

"Were we ever enemies?"

"Only strangers."

We start laughing again and, to my horror, there are no taps on the roof. *How fuckin' dumb*, I thought. We're retarded now. "Hey. How's your infection?"

"Fine," he said and his head fell forward. "Thank you for asking."

"Did you really have your period?"

He smiled. "There is power in deception." He turned to me with his eyes closed. "Was it you or Brian who fucked up my pills?"

I looked at him dead in the eye. "Me." We burst out laughing.

"Ah." He bowed. "Your strategy of sabotage worked well."

"What happens when you're better?" I dry swallowed.

He was going through his pockets. "I have gum. What do you mean?"

"Will we fight again?"

He made the motion of holding an arrow and snapping it over his knee. "This is us alone." He then motioned that he was holding a quiver of arrows. He motioned that he was trying to break it over his knee but couldn't. "This is us together." He held his right hand in front of his face and made a splashing motion with his hand while staring at it. "Dust in the wind."

I started laughing. I'd seen this in a hundred movies and he looked stupid acting it out—then I remembered: "I wanted to kill him," I say.

"Who?"

"The principal." I nod. "I made a promise to protect her."

"I figured you were different." He shrugged. "I'm a Newfie. My dad's a cop. I have an inner ear infection. My eardrum almost popped because of you. That's all. What do I have?"

"There's only four Dogribs in PWS. Well, five including her."

"Don't kill him," he said suddenly.

I looked at him closely. "Why?"

"They say if you wait long enough, the body of your enemy will float by you down the river."

I stop. Look at him. "What's the story?"

"I read it somewhere. East Indians, I think."

"Where'd you read this?"

"Library," he says. This filled me with something sweet. It was a soft power that rose from inside me. Is this wisdom or smoke?

I think about this and say, "You have given me strength."

"As have you. Tell me," he asked. "What is your faith?"

I looked at him. "What do you mean?"

"You have the peace pipe, don't you?"

I started to laugh. "That's the Crees."

He started to laugh so hard he snorted. "Well, what are we doing this for?"

I couldn't stop laughing. I laughed so hard I actually slid off the fibreglass. "It was your idea."

He reached over and handed me gum. "Was it?"

I started to float, felt like. I looked at the gum in its wrapper and had no idea how to open it. "Okay okay. We take from the best."

"From what?"

"Well," I say, "we have our own ceremonies. Like we feed the fire. We have rat root. We pray."

"Go to church?"

I nodded. "But we don't believe in original sin."

"How's that?"

"No guilt."

"What?" He pulled me up.

"Jesus didn't die for me. You're gonna tell me Wendy or your little sister was born with sin?"

"Go on."

"Why live in fear and shame?"

"God doesn't make junk." He nodded. "Give me that." He unwrapped the gum I had and put it in my mouth.

"So where is she now?"

"What?"

"Where is Wendy now?"

I closed my eyes. "Home. With our grandma."

"Shouldn't you be there?"

I shook my head and started rocking. "I can't... I can't face them."

"So you'll kill the principal and go to jail and never see them again?"

I pressed the palms of my hands into my eyes. "I don't know what to do."

"You're, what, sixteen? Why not let the cops and judges do what they're supposed to do?"

I looked at him and he looked back. He was being totally serious. Maybe he was right. I felt lighter when he said that, like maybe it wasn't all my problem.

"Are you sure the Dogribs don't use the peace pipe?" he asked.

I let my breath out. "I don't know...."

"Sorry I called you a harelip," Marvin blurted in a whisper and looked away.

I stopped mid blink. My head snapped up. "It's better than cunt mouth." I looked at the northern lights. They were growing now. I could whistle with my sharp teeth and call them if I wanted to.

"I'd like to help you," he said quietly. I looked at him and he was trembling. "I'd like to help you," he said again. "Let's go bless that house." I nodded and thought of his dead sister. Had he ever put her to rest? Marvin looked at me with concern in his eyes. He did not stare at my lip, and so we left for the rape house.

I remember my promise. My contract. Ehtsi spoke English so softly. "*Sah*, you will go to where the school is. In Fort Simmer. The principal has agreed to adopt Wendy. He met her this week. She's your cousin. You will protect her."

I looked at her and Wendy smiled, rolling her eyes up and to the right. That meant she was happy. To the left meant she was scared. Her eyes were to the left a lot before she left because the by-law officer had started hunting her. He even chased her into the bush a few days before, but she knew to hide. This man was the son of the chief, so we couldn't say nothing.

"Education," Grandma said, "is what you need these days for work. It makes you strong like two people."

"I'll protect her, Ehtsi," I said. "I promise."

I was given two boxes filled with rat root, dry meat, dry fish, and pemmican. I finally felt like a man. I had wanted to be there for Wendy when we moved here, but I wasn't. The truth was it was a relief to not have to worry about my cousin and watch her all the time. The principal never invited me over to his house once I came to town. I got caught up in school. I'd see Wendy, happy and wandering. I knew she was okay. I trusted. *You were the principal. You had a wife.*

Marvin doubled. In my T-shirt, I raced with Marvin down Main Street and now as we stand outside the rape house, I think of what Marvin said, about the body of your enemy floating down the river. Maybe he's right. Maybe I don't have to kill my contract. Maybe the Creator or jail has something worse for him. I have heard that Wendy is back in Fort Rae, safe with Ehtsi. Mending. I'm sure they're wondering when I'll return.

"Can we pray for my sister?" Marvin asks as the smoke blankets me.

"Sure," I say.

I hold the rat root up and he puts his hands over it, to catch some of the smoke. He then washes his body with it, over and over, turning and turning. He washes his face with it; then his hands; his mouth. He must have learned this from the Crees, I think. That's how they smudge.

"You?" he asks.

I shake my head. This is not our way.

I don't pray to God here. I pray to our ancestors who knew how to purify where someone had died or suffered. I pray to our mother who gave birth to six dog pups.

I look at Marvin and nod. We then start walking around the house as the little stick called rat root smokes and smokes. We circle the house without talking and it hits me halfway through that Marvin is praying. It's the Lord's Prayer and then a few Hail Mary's in whispers.

I would leave to go home as soon as I could to be with Ehtsi and Wendy, but why did I have the sense that this was not finished? Torchy had made up his mind about something. I could see it. Feel it. Perhaps he and Sfen would take care of the principal.

I think of the blueprints for a room I will design. I will design it for Wendy in my mind only. It will be a room for night angels. People from all over the world will go there. Into the room you enter. In darkness. You can hear breathing. There are angels hunched and waiting

there with folded wings. Waiting with their mouths and their deep-
est wishes for you. Their perfect mouths are open and waiting. And
you enter. And the room pulls you away from yourself. And you feel
with your hands for the perfect mouth for you. And you can kiss and
kiss and kiss. With tongue. With breath. You can kiss angels forever.
You can kiss until you faint. You can kiss until you're clean. You can
kiss as many mouths as you hunger for, and the angels will never stop
being there, and you can kiss every filthy thing away. And in this room
stands Wendy. She is standing in the middle. She is surrounded with
the angel-light of herself as we surround the rape house with the light
of two. She is standing there with her own sweet smile holding the
small hand of Marvin's little sister. Angels will protect them always.
And from there my cousin's light will glow.

And there my love will be...

Feeding the Fire

FROM THE SHADOWS OF THE SPRUCE TREES, WE WAITED UNTIL the last of the trucks passed while Sfen stood with two slop pails full of sawdust. I held two jerry cans filled with leaded gasoline. Each one was mixed with flour for a little bit of stick.

"Ready, Torch?"

I nodded. Then we made our way up the cul-de-sac with our workboots crunching anything under us. That crunching reminded me of the night I had my arm broken by my mom's boyfriend. That was the last time I let anyone touch me. Me and Sfen signatured a few hematomas across his head, and I know my mom's ex — years later now — thinks of us every morning when he has to put his teeth in. We always had a Plan B for him and, sure enough, we got a Plan B for Mister Principal when he comes back tomorrow for his trial. Our faces were painted with bear grease and dog blood because of it.

The moon was full and we'd shot out all the street lights around the house with dusk-feathered arrows. Revenge soon and I was thinking about how most girls start to menstruate when they hit 105 pounds. I wondered if the principal kept our cousin at 104. I was thinking about how when the doctor was mixing my cast, he told me that when a bone's broke, the body circles a ring around it and after it heals, it's the strongest part of the body. That's what happened to us, I thought, with the residential schools and all the rape and grief that followed after. Mister Principal was no different: just another white man in a long line of takers. There's a circle around all of us now and no one will ever touch us again. Warriors make sure of that.

But who calls the warriors forward? Is it the Creator? The land? Those who can't fight back? The sinners or the sinned against?

We'd told our apostles, "Leave your mark on every home you were touched or raped in. Leave it with a handprint and we'll take care of the rest." As we came around the back of his house, we saw all of the recent renovations on the principal's property: a new deck, new fencing. They say Wendy needed stitches for what he did to her, and he'd need a lot more than that after we were done with him.

Sfen handed me some well-worn work gloves out of his packsack as I produced an axe handle out of mine. I then rolled up my sleeves to reveal the tattoos my bro had given me for my birthday. The tattoos were crosses and two words had been carved into the bone-meat of my arms. When facing a mirror, with my arms in a cross, you could read the words: "Dogrib Forever."

"Tell me again how God cleans?" I asked Sfen, for every time my bro said it I got the shivers from head to toe.

"With fire, brother," he smiled. "Our god cleans with fire." We were godless but loyal to heaven and the handcuff key that I kept in the hem of my sock started to heat up. In fact, it started to burn with the promise of unleashing Plan B on the principal tomorrow. I started to shiver with the thought of us burning every marked house in town down to the ground tonight. There were more than one hundred handprints on the doors here in the village of the child hunters.

You see there was an island where we put all the dogs that bite children. They hadn't eaten for a week. I looked forward to saying, "We have brought you something to kill," when we turned the principal loose on the island of his kidnapping. That was gonna be stellar, practically Biblical.

"Whatcha thinkin' about?" Sfen asked.

"Some people need killin'," I said. I then proceeded to smash in all of the principal's windows while Sfen nodded and calmly lit a smoke....

Afterwords

On the Wings of this Prayer
This was written in Pangnirtung in the summer of 2010 when I ventured to Nunavut for the very first time. When the Wheetago return let it be the old ways that save us. This story is for everyone in Pangnirtung. I love your community so much. Thank you for sharing your wisdom and spirit with me. I could not have written "On the Wings of this Prayer" without the inspiration of Sherman Alexie. *Mahsi cho*, Sherman. Thank you, as well, to Michael Callaghan of Exile Editions for publishing it in the CVC *Anthology—Book One* upon being selected as one of ten stories shortlisted for the Gloria Vanderbilt/Exile Short Fiction Competition in 2011; he also printed it in volume 35, no. 4 of *Exile: The Literary Quarterly*.

The Fleshing
This is a "what if?" story that I was asked to write by Dr. Pamela Sing for a Rougarou anthology she's working on for the University of Alberta Press. In 1866, Father Émile Petitot transcribed a story told to him in the NWT by a Dene man of a shape-shifting man who, the night of his marriage to a woman of the "Copper people" or Yellowknives, reveals his true nature. Petitot's French translation was published in 1886. I was asked to modernize this encounter. What would you do if you entered a room where a Wheetago had taken hostages and you were passed a note: Don't let it make the sound? I want to dedicate this story to Edna Beaver, Earl Evans and Irene Sanderson for terrifying me with Wheetago stories. Eee!

Children of the Sundance

I love this story because it solidifies why Clarence and Brutus are so close in stories like "Let's Beat the Shit Out of Herman Rosko" in *Angel Wing Splash Pattern*; "Dogrib Midnight Runners" in *The Moon of Letting Go* and "Love Song" in this collection. This is a going back in time story and I'm so looking forward to writing more about this trinity of brothers, friends and streaking warriors.

Tony Toenails

Ha ha, you know how they say the rumours are always true in Indian Country? Well, this is based on a true story and was a hoot to write. It was published in *Up Here*'s December, 2011 issue. This is for every-body in Fort Smith because without all y'all, I wouldn't be me.

Love Song

This was the first short story I ever published. It appeared in *Descant*: Vol. 24, No. 3, Fall 1993. I've tweaked "Love Song" a bit for this collection, and I'd like to dedicate this story to Ivan Coyote because Ivan makes me want to be a better storyteller all the time. I can't wait for you to read the new stories I'm planning for Grant, Clarence and Brutus. There is so much magic coming their way. I know I call them streaking warriors, but they're more than that: they're prayer warriors. They just don't know it yet.

Devotion

Dedicated to Mr. Chris Trott who inspired this story. Also, with thanks to the people of Pangnirtung. I want to thank Bill Street for working on this with me as we performed it for the public in January of 2011 along with sixteen superb musicians all playing along for a public performance at the University of Alberta. Thank you to the editors of *Prairie Fire* for publishing it in their special issue "Boreality: Listening to the Heart of the Forest" (33.1, spring 2012).

Lizard People
I love this planet and her people and, sometimes, you just have to laugh and give thanks for the abundance and hilarity that surrounds us all right now. This story is for Omer and Jennie.

Godless but Loyal to Heaven
You've met Torchy before in "Mermaids," published in *Angel Wing Splash Pattern*. I've always wondered what happened to him, Stephanie and Snowbird six months after, and this is their story. I'd like to dedicate this to all my brothers: Roger, Jamie, Johnny, James, Mike, Jon Liv, Junior, Marty and Trevor.

The Contract
Anyone who knows me knows I'm working on a novel called *Sword of Antlers*. This is the perfect excerpt behind the novel that introduces Bear from "The Fleshing." He's my new gladiator and if anyone can defeat a Wheetago and walk a path that leads to forgiveness, it's him. This story was published in *Exile*'s spring issue in 2012. I'd like to give thanks to Mary Koyina Richardson for her wisdom on how to purify a haunted place using traditional Tlicho medicine. *Mahsi cho*, Mary! I'd like to dedicate this to Niigaanwewidam James Sinclair because he inspires me so much.

Mahsi cho for reading my stories. I am indebted to the University of Alberta's Writer-in-Residence program, where I was Writer in Residence for 2011–2012. Thank you for welcoming me to Edmonton with so much respect and community. I'd also like to thank Lee Maracle for sharing with me that in writing we can find what has been stolen, repair what has been disfigured, and heal what has been damaged. *Mahsi cho*, Lee. Your words guide me every day.

A huge *mahsi cho* to my editor, Maurice Mierau, and my agent, Janine Cheeseman. Thank you!

Dreams are contagious and this collection is a dream come true for me. Thank you for sharing this with me, and may these dreams and stories inspire you with your own.

Thank you to everyone who believes in me. You bring me strength and grace. *Mahsi cho.*